A Season in Queens

JOANNE & GERRY DRYANSKY

A SEASON in QUEENS

NEW YORK

LONDON • NASHVILLE • MELBOURNE • VANCOUVER

A Season in Queens

Publisher's Note: This novel is a work of fiction. Names, characters, places, and incidents are either products of the author's imagination or used fictitiously. All characters are fictional, and any similarity to people living or dead is purely coincidental.

Published in New York, New York, by Morgan James Publishing. Morgan James is a trademark of Morgan James, LLC. www.MorganJamesPublishing.com

ISBN 9781631954528 paperback
ISBN 9781631954535 eBook
Library of Congress Control Number: 2020951050

Cover Design by:
Megan Dillon
megan@creativeninjadesigns.com

Interior Design by:
Christopher Kirk
www.GFSstudio.com

N.B.: The time and place of this story are as real as any. While they are true to the life then and there, the people are not based on anyone who lived. Erin, who sets forth in our novel to make a novel of her memory enriched by her imagination, is someone who never existed, either. Our hope is that, with the revelatory power of storytelling, she lives.
—J&G Dryansky

Morgan James is a proud partner of Habitat for Humanity Peninsula and Greater Williamsburg. Partners in building since 2006.

Get involved today! Visit
MorganJamesPublishing.com/giving-back

For André, Larisa, and Ruth

Acknowledgments

Our acknowledgments go to David Hancock and Jim Howard, dauntless in their dedication to what they achieve, to Cortney Donelson and her sensitive vision, along with Bonnie Rauch, Taylor Chaffer, and the keen crew at Morgan James, kindest of shepherds.

Try to be one of the people on whom nothing is lost!
—Henry James
from *The Art of Fiction*

ONE

A plague was abroad in America, but we were buoyed with hope, coming back from years of calamity. In the sun porch windows on 240th Street in Cambria Heights, little banners were still there with their gold stars, emblems of cheerless pride, pathetic titles to the ownership of loss. Day by day, year after year, the neighbors had all been bound by their exalted determination, ripping out lawns and flowers to plant vegetables, selling each other Victory Bonds, gathering scrap metal piled at the end of the street for the Victory Effort, and even giving the butcher over on Linden Boulevard back fat that was supposed to become nitroglycerin. Did anyone imagine that their meat scraps would destroy Dresden? Did any of them shed a tear with the thought? While night after night, during those long years, people everywhere in the nation bedded down, one by one, with their personal fears and memories, to their personal nightmares.

They'd come out of it together in their pride and grief. Wounded lives, buoyed at the same time by the fulfillment of victory. And that proof of their fortitude in the worst of times seemed to augur a rebirth of better ones, almost like a hoped-for truth about the world, like the rationality of redemption.

They'd been hit with an understanding of what the world could truly be beyond their little lower-middle class haven of life, liberty, and the pursuit of happiness—a hit like the destruction of a bunker. But it was 1946, and the War was months over. And the years just before it of the anxious insecurity or the despair and deprivation of the Great Depression were behind as well. They were ready to move on.

Into the sunlight.

Few people then and even now may have heard of Cambria Heights, even New Yorkers. Nothing that caused a stir in the rest of the world ever seemed to have happened out there at the far end of Queens, a bus ride, and then a subway ride, an hour and a half of journeying to what people in Cambria then called "The City": Manhattan. Unless you take account of Louis "Lepke" Buchalter, the celebrated CEO of Murder Incorporated, hunted by police and politicians, who had been another embodiment of a world of violence beyond that neighborhood and at the same time the street's celebrity. He had found clandestine nights of refuge at the Siegals' (his in-laws) house on 240th Street. That was shortly before he was tricked into surrendering with the treacherous enticement of leniency, by Walter Winchell the star of radio news, and subsequently electrocuted, two years earlier than the spring of 1946.

In the 1920s, "Cambria Heights" must have sounded classy to the builders—in a nation still in awe of things that evoked England. Movie stars spoke stage English like Oxfordians. The builders here, piece by piece, defying the advent of the Depression, converted empty lots and patches of farmland into symmetrical rows of streets, with almost identical little brick houses whose facades were inspired by the style of English manors. In midget imitations. No one knows what brought the Cambria Title and Savings Bank of Cambria County, Pennsylvania to the far edge of Queens, New York, to create this retreat, as its real estate prospectus put it, "for working families and civil servants who wanted to leave the city." The name, which brought to mind social ascendance, was also motivated literally by geography. Cambria Heights sits uphill from a plain called Queens Village, fifty feet above sea level, to be exact, on a land grant that Peter Stuyvesant gave to farmers in 1655. Not far away, the last glacier of the Ice Age stopped advancing, leaving a furrow of gravel near Cunningham Park, 385 acres of greenery, preserved during the Depression as a good place amid all that was bad, for the people to picnic at tables built by the W.P.A. Cambria Heights touches the border of Nassau County, near the Belmont racetrack named after an immigrant who changed his surname to a more patrician-sounding version of Schönberg, while rising to great wealth in the Nineteenth Century, fulfilling an American dream.

The people who came to live in Cambria Heights after it was "developed" were dreamers too. It was where, as put more precisely than in the Bank's prospectus, people who managed to have jobs during the Depression were able to leave behind the tenements of the city. Though Cambria was part of New York City's Borough of Queens, "The City," Manhattan, was from where they'd migrated, as if from another, much harsher country, to the locus of their aspirations of a decent life. A lot of them were firemen, a lot of others policemen; they were craftsmen, plumbers, electricians. On 240th Street, Billy Nowak, who drove his truck through the night five nights a week distributing bundles of the *New York Daily News* to dealers clear to the tip of Long Island at Montauk Point, told Dr. Lyons, when all that rattling had made him a lumbago patient of the newly arrived physician, about the day in 1938 when he and Wanda—they'd lived in a walk-up in Brownsville—went to the bank in Springfield Gardens with five hundred dollars to put down on their four-thousand dollar house, and walked to Jamaica for the subway back to Brooklyn, with just a quarter plus the two nickels for the ride, between them till payday.

Brian and Sally Burke, who brought me into the world as a native child of Cambria in 1928, had bought their house that year. He was managing a good living working for a window maker, who had contracts with Cambria's builders. He liked the house he saw and so did my mother, a registered nurse.

In Cambria Heights, crocuses, then pansies, tulips, and daffodils would flower with the start of spring outside the sun porches, signaling that screens would soon replace storm windows. White, pink, and pale blue snowball bushes and azaleas blossomed. At night, in the backyards, while the season warmed in increments of summer, rosebuds opened and scented the air, sprinklers hissed like domesticated snakes, and fireflies flashed among the people cooling off in the yards behind their houses, deep in their slatted, painted, wooden garden chairs, while others, still following the habits of the city that they'd left, sat on their front stoops. A half-hour bus ride beyond the end of the IND subway in Jamaica, Cambria Heights was, for its residents, the ultimate episode of realized dreams, before each of their allotments of time ran out.

Buying into Cambria, you got your own neat and solid little brick domain, your lawn, and your backyard with room for your kids' swing and a barbecue. You would also have your church.

The Pastor James King Sr.'s Methodist Church was just down the street on 240th, near 111th Avenue. We Catholics were of a much larger congregation at Sacred Heart, the flock of Father Gerry Maloney. A gingerly tolerance that was neighborliness prevailed over the unrepressed differences.

In the end, despite their shared aspirations, differences would deeply trouble the privileged life of 240th Street in Cambria Heights.

It would change when a Black war hero arrived, alien from their self-sufficiency—testing who they were at heart as human beings in the world—and again on the day that I saw Dr. Cato Lyons lying on the floor of his examination room, his head bashed in. And when my own life had already been direly changed…

꧁

This was the world that I was born into in the fall of 1928. To a mother whose maternal love would fit the care and devotion of a true nurse, and a loving father, the straightest of what cynical people came to call "straight arrows." Cambria was the material enclave of his modest optimism over how the world could be good, and in goodness was his simple faith, unscathed by the great Crash the year after I became a treasured part of his life. Looking back, although my father was not a very religious protestant of the Northern Ireland Burkes—he'd become a Catholic for my mother—he might still have come to feel something like being, as Calvin put it, "elected," modestly though, with a secure job making windows when men of his generation would be selling apples and warming their hands-on street fires. In any case, he never gave us to believe that predestination was involved in his faith—and he would not go gently to the bottom of the sea, not long after he left us, when each of our three lives were torn asunder.

All the moralists on earth haven't ever made the case that a person is one thing. My father Brian was driven by a sort of exultation of patriotism, and with that, I have to believe, a tormented yearning for self-fulfillment. He loved me, would carry me on his shoulders all over until my legs were much too long, and spoiled me with treats and toys. He'd have me choose his ties—with, he'd said, my born taste—when he and mother went out to a restaurant treat, or a party with friends like them.

And he abandoned me. I have to say it as I felt it: deeply and with anger. I have to add that a kind of profound, maybe malignant, boredom haunted him and drove him to leave. I think it was actually the monotony of gestures that was his job—not a true, fulfilling craft, but one empty of an artisan's creativity. It was what he had been able to keep doing and earning in those body and soul threatening times. It protected and enclosed him in some kind of bubble of spiritual emptiness, which he suffered for the payoff of the one incomparably thrilling choice of his life, my mother.

My mother and my father had been so powerfully in love that at times I felt that I, the only child my mother would bear, was a needless presence. Despite the affection they both lavished on me, I couldn't help but feel in a sense adrift outside of their idyll. Or on a very small island. Their love showed in a glance, in hands reaching across the table at dinner, in an exchange of reverential looks, in a touch of closeness that needed nothing apparent at the moment to inspire it.

And he left her. Left us. Off to sea and a war that hadn't even started yet, though he had convinced himself into certainty that it was coming. Years later I would remember what Jimmy King would say after D-Day: "I don't want it all to be over before I got my chance." Brian left before it began, and it was over for him the day it did begin, on that other never-forgettable date in our history, that "will live in infamy."

My mother never once blamed him for leaving; she loved him and mourned him with bottomless grief. The vengeance that would drive her made his mission hers...

≈

My mother Sally once asked: "What do you really want to do when you get out of Barnard?" She'd come home from the Pacific—come back into my life, after the years when my grand-mother Iris and I were alone together in our complicity. It was a day not long before the end of my freshman year at Barnard College. It was awkward, sitting there in Manhattan in a Shraffts Café, over chicken à la king, while couples of East Side groomed women at other tables exchanged hushed disclosures about others who weren't there. With her absence, my mother and I had lost the intimacy between mother and child of my early years; I felt a gap that was hard to jump over, and now we weren't living together. I was flustered to tell her that I intended to write—to be a writer. I'd confided, and almost wished I hadn't. She worried over the risk. I felt small revealing my self-centered ambition, sitting across from her. She sipped her iced tea through a straw and recreated a noise like one I'd make when I was a little girl. That wink of complicity actually made me feel worse: There was lipstick on her straw. I saw a tiny imprint of a person's existence. And no one lives forever. After all the fearful incertitude she'd known, could I fault her over fear of the odds of what my life might become?

My mother was bright, sensitive, and irrefutably brave, but she did not have perilous personal aspirations. She'd given of herself, done her war valiantly out of dedication not ambition, driven unambiguously to what she believed was a higher level of behaving. She named it vengeance.

So, in my own little precarious way, I began these pages, the ones I saved in my diary and wrote afterward, on that tightrope from word to word, with those moments when the way forward freezes as if emptiness looms and can swallow you up. For a long time, I was inhibited by the thought that it was indiscreet or even conscienceless to recount this whole story. But it's there as a fateful moment in my life, and this is all about then, filled out with the lives that I have made grow into a paradigm of life in my own mind, with fragments that I'd heard—most of all from my grandmother, who was the confidante for so many people on our street.

Selling her Victory Bonds door to door, talking a long time to people with the charm in her caring. As much as she was a militant patriot, she was a pilgrim of her fellow-feeling. People fascinated my grandmother: She understood so many stories, their beginnings and middles, and many of their endings on earth, until her own came, with very old age, serenely, as if in awe of anticipating a great disclosure.

I would learn that she'd be a consolation to Jimmy King's gentle, timid mother in her days of grief and worry, when Jimmy had come home to Cambria the way he was then.

My grandmother Iris was, in all, never a banal gossip, and I believe that she shared her confidences with no one else but me. As if she could foresee, like Dr. Franklin, with the typewriter he gifted me, that I, in my way, might turn out to be the heiress of her high curiosity.

I will always see in my mind the Western Union teenager coasting into our lives on a bicycle, wearing that uniform that they wore then, with riding pants. His military outfit made him look like an envoy of the elsewhere my father had gone, brimming with angry patriotism and as I'd come to sense afterward—faring forth for self-fulfillment. By December 7th, our lawns and doors had been decorated for Christmas, the season of goodwill and cheer.

My mother read the telegram as if it might just not be what she already understood; she shrieked and fell stiffly to the floor and then her tears flowed with a silence more awesome than sound. I was frightened and powerless to do anything to help her, while my own grief overpowered me, with no one there at that moment to console me. The messenger fled. Finally, mother got herself up and went into my parents' bedroom, unable to speak, and shut the door. I was old enough to respond to my only cogent thought and pick up the phone and call Grandma Iris.

I waited in the dark, alone in the living room. Night had fallen before the lights of an arriving car, in which Grandma's neighbor, a Mrs. Pult, had driven her from her apartment in Brooklyn, lit a living room wall.

Grandma held me before she knocked on her daughter's door. I heard them speaking. My mother came out with a look of anger beyond grief. She had, I think, silently taken the vow of her mission behind that door.

She came out of their bedroom—I see it still—wearing my father's jacket, and crying no more.

I wasn't in a state to go back to school for weeks. To face anyone but Jimmy…

ఞ

It may no longer be hard to believe that close friendships like ours between a boy and a girl could be driven by anything other than sex. Jimmy was like the older brother I never had. Two years ahead of me in school, in a sense paving a way, an inspiration: the outstanding athlete who was also an exceptional scholar. We were soulmates, if you will, of intellectual aspirations. Since I was in fifth grade and he in the seventh, we would walk to school, to P.S. 147 together. My mother, with my father's accord, had put me in public school separate from the other Catholic kids at Sacred Heart. As a child, she had been taken out of Catholic school by her own mother for reasons that she never would express. From the time that I was very young, I'd be shy, and in ways, Jimmy was also my protector. There were wild kids in the neighborhood, in particular the twin Irish Sullivan brothers from a ramshackle house near the remaining vacant lots in Cambria. A year older than Jimmy but no bigger. I, in my school, was for them an apostate, and one snowy Ash Wednesday, when I was coming home from school with a clean forehead unlike theirs, Billie hit me with a snowball covering a rock. Jimmy knocked him to the ground, and pushed his head in the snow, while Bobbie ran away.

He knew how to fight.

When he went on to Andrew Jackson High School I'd felt a little lost. He'd grown into another world, without looking back to P.S. 147. He was very popular. Girls, I'd heard, ran after him. I was still an awkward kid, with freckles, red hair, and a wiry pony tail, and he had his pompadour, even features, and a lithe build already from swimming. By junior year he would be the best swimmer in memory at Jackson.

I'd felt a little outpaced by him on the trajectory of his life, but when I came to Jackson myself, the following year, the bond we'd felt would prevail…

჻

Then he left.

The day after D-Day, June 6, 1944, Jimmy, who'd turned eighteen, decided not to wait to attend his graduation that month. Jimmy hurried on the Q4 bus to Jamaica and went to the Army recruiting office to sign up. When he came home his mother could not hold back tears.

"I don't want it all to be over before I got my chance."

His father didn't show distress. Almost without reflection, the awareness came to him that his son was a man and that his gesture was a man's decision. He should not argue against it with his fears from what he himself had known, however they beset him. He repressed them and at where things now lay, he said, with a final edge of disapproval, he would have hoped that Jimmy had chosen the Marines.

Jimmy said that he'd get out of basic training faster than with the Marines. He got his wish.

He came home five weeks later. From Camp Kilmer.

"I'm on a twenty-four-hour pass," he said. He actually looked at his watch, as we sat down together on the swing of my backyard. He was ebullient. "We're shipping out right afterward."

Camp Gruber, Oklahoma, he said, had been no big ordeal. A lot of the guys were really out of shape and what they were telling him was "intensive training" was not any harder than what he'd known on the swimming team. "We were in the barracks they had the kraut prisoners in," he said, "and you can still smell them. Guess I'll be smelling a lot more of them soon."

The base was a thirty-four-cent bus ride away from a town

called Mushogee, where, for a quarter, the bars served white light-ening from under the counter—served according to local custom in mason jars—and there were nice, proper families as well that would invite the boys to eat at home with them.

"No matter how it sounds to you, Erin, Mushogee is a lot like Cambria. At the base we're guys from all over the country.

"We're going to show them America."

I remembered that my father had been just as excited. I couldn't hold back my worry, but I just couldn't express it. Jimmy and I were close friends since grammar school who lived across the street from each other, close, with that special com-plicity as the very bright ones at school. What good, anyway, would there be for me to caution him, as if my caution could in any way be a shield where he was going? I listened while dread came over me irrepressibly. When he read my face, I nodded and smiled, with a contrived reassurance, but I didn't even know how to express a right goodbye…

Jimmy's few letters came from overseas with blackened pas-sages by the censors: places blackened out. Forbidden mentions of destinations. Black that itself made known that the unsaid was deeply dark. It covered his pages that said almost nothing else.

With the letter from the 14th Combat Support Hospital in Gar-misch, came the confirmation that his war in Europe was over.

Two years had passed since I last saw him. I remembered what he looked like the day I'd seen him leaving home. He'd come to say goodbye at my doorstep. He looked flushed with enthusiasm, and I actually felt a little hurt that it showed more than any remorse about our parting. He gave me a fraternal hug that brought on the honk of a horn. I saw the car, his parents waiting. His father gave a second honk that sounded like irritation, and Jimmy turned and hurried off. They were driving him to the Long Island Railroad, where he'd change for Grand Central Station, and the rest of the world...

TWO

t was the last homecoming block party on 240th Street. Jimmy, who had been hospitalized in an unpronounceable town in Germany before France, was coming home to Cambria.

The neighbors had already welcomed back their heroes, while some of them, like my father, who'd been in the engine room of the U.S.S. Arizona at Pearl Harbor, were never coming home. But a banner strung across the street from tree to tree in red, white, and blue crepe paper read, "Welcome Home Jimmy."

A long table near a wooden dance floor was crowded with cold cuts, potato salad, coleslaw, baked macaroni, angel food cake, and a variety of pies. Beverages options included two kegs of Trommer's White Label and bottles of cream soda and root beer. Food rationing had just ended and all that seemed all the more munificent in reviving memories of deprivation.

Someone in charge of a Victrola put on Frank Sinatra singing "What is America to Me." I heard "all races and religions."

Those lyrics would echo to me at a time soon ahead with sad irony.

Meanwhile, that golden voice filled the air. People went silent, holding their breath, as if, with some transformative magic, it brightened the sunlight. Until the needle jumped its last groove and scratched and turned until someone put the Victrola out of its agony, and a blast of rhythm came on: Bing Crosby and The Andrew Sisters' "Accentuate the Positive." People jumped up and danced and danced, as if enacting the positive—as if dancing away years of anguish and calamity...

17

They stopped when what they'd been waiting for happened, as Pastor King's gray Packard pulled up. From inside the Kings' house Moe began to bark excitedly, as if the dog could smell his family's car through the front door.

Pastor King and Mrs. King stepped out and blinked at the sun. They both looked strangely like two people who might have been sleeping sitting up on a train until they were dropped off somewhere they'd never been before; Mrs. King's disoriented gaze fixed suddenly on, "Welcome Home Jimmy," and she wiped a corner of her eye.

Someone shouted "Jimmy!"

Dr. King squared his shoulders.

He said: "Jimmy has had a serious problem…of transportation. He's on his way. He'd be happy if you went on celebrating for him."

No Jimmy…

No Jimmy. I stood at the edge of the dance floor, alone, with no appetite for the food. I made my way across the street toward my house. I'd thought that even there in public, our greeting each other for the first time since he'd gone away would be a cherished moment, eye to eye, minds brimming with memories. But Jimmy—my best friend who'd once called me his soulmate—had gone into another world and was still somewhere else. And I would come to sense that he wasn't there for me, or anyone really.

I stopped in the street and waited another moment, as if I could believe that Jimmy would appear after all, like some magician's show trick, and when I looked back, I saw Pastor King square his shoulders and walk with something like a military gait toward his house. And then Mrs. King, standing all alone for a moment beside the Packard, made a wan smile and followed him. They went in, and nobody came out. The lights in the house went off. People looked a little sheepish.

The party was over.

After dark, from the window of my bedroom, I saw a cab pull up. Under the streetlight, he came out in a uniform bent over with a heavy duffel bag on his shoulder. Hunched, with a bleak face, Jimmy went into his house with his burden. The light went out over his door.

Welcome home, Jimmy…

I had seen Pastor King's look flicker between grief and anger.

∾

The Reverend Dr. King, as suited his calling, might have been presumed to be an openly compassionate person, but that wasn't obvious. He was a man with a very conflicted nature. He did kind things that the ministers of a church were accustomed to do. For example, he reached out to the youngsters in his congregation by coaching a Cub Scout softball team. He collected clothing for the poor. He had been an athlete himself, and when Wilson declared war on Germany, he turned his back without hesitation at being a college boy in a school for the well-off. (His father was a banker, and he grew up in Short Hills, New Jersey, before the banker sent him off to The Hill School and then Amherst.) Having been a champion college boxer, he hoped to enrich an already illustrious definition of himself: a hero for his country. He volunteered for the Marines. And so, he came to find himself in hell on earth. He'd fought bravely and survived in the slaughter at Belleau Wood. The horror he'd lived through changed his life; his reaction to it was to become a pastor. It was more a decision of the mind than of the heart. He desperately needed an explanation of what made the world what it is—a definition and a path to move forward. He needed a calm and bright place to keep out of his consciousness what strange, awful things he'd known.

Belleau Wood: Jimmy had heard his whole story. More than once. When the 1st Battalion of the Sixth Marine Regiment, of which his father had been a Lieutenant, was reduced to a tenth of its strength and King was the last commissioned officer standing, while sergeants and even corporals led the bayonet charges that finally broke the German lines and—with little food, pitifully little water, and so short of sleep that men fell into slumber under bombardment—the Marines crushed the counter attack of an over-whelming force. By then, they were something other than human. They reattacked wearing masks in fear of mustard gas, foaming at the mouth, moving on all fours. *Teufelhunde!* the frightened Germans screamed. "Devil dogs."

He came back changed, a little like Saul on the road from Tarsus to Damascus—but all that violence was still a scar on his psyche. He kept trying to live according to an abstraction of good-ness, having damaged his spontaneity of emotions. His faith was something that gave his thoughts clear borders. As in battle, his mind's greatest asset was self-control while as if anger and compassion were protagonists of his unending inner war.

⁓

Thunder broke open Jimmy's sleep. He bolted awake and reached for his rifle. It wasn't there. The bed was soft and smelled of freshly washed sheets. His sweat had soaked a crisp, white top sheet. Reality was not the hole in the ground. His mind had been there, dreaming of the real place in the past. Now: he was awake and this good past became the now world.

The clock beside his bed said it was still the middle of the night. His window was dark. He pulled the top sheet over his head, and when he dozed again, he was back again in his nightmare…

⁓

Across the street, in my sleep, I heard Jimmy's voice, having read and reread the letter from the hospital in Germany. He'd written:

"Well, Erin, I'm alive, hard to believe, and I expect to make it to my nineteenth birthday. I have made—should I have said crawled?—my way out of the world that I couldn't write you about, as if censors could black it out of my mind in blacking out letters. I have to tell it, forgive the details. It's an education about life, like a fall from grace as my devout father might put it. It's a twisting mirror of the world we think we know, but it's no illusion, no mirage. Yeah, a circus mirror. What a circus.

"Guys who were there weren't there anymore. You woke up, had a kind of breakfast, expecting a day of the same. The horrors you saw, people torn open, was normal, the givens, the contents of any day's experience. You get an education about what we are when you see someone shot open. It seems something alien. We'd never seen it before, but that ugly accumulation of soft matter is our poor, mortal us. As for the rest of our bearings, so to speak, this was where we were and that was what was there, and you accepted it like breathing. Until it was as if something exploded—not around you this time, but in your brain—and you fell through that metaphorical crater down into another, private world. And that alienation was a refuge. Another place of virtual, alternate realities. A kaleidoscope of uninvited, unexpected chimeras that come on like beliefs. To the point of confusion where, faced with what we do, something happens like a disbelief in reality.

"But my body is intact, thank the Lord, as my Pop would say. When we were fighting, we were walking most of the time, and with the winter, our feet were soaked in the snow. As the least of our worries, our boots were inadequate, to use a polite word about whomever got the contract for them.

"The Rainbow division, where they'd put me had lost a lot of men since 1944. It's a kind of elite group, full of grit and spirit. It got its name in 1917, when it was put together with National Guards units from all over America.

"You remember that I told you how much I wanted to have been there at D-day when we hit the beach, but now I know I was lucky to have been spared that assault—essentially no different from when armies attacked fortresses with bows and arrows and kept on going forward. You must get a different perception of glory when people are falling and literally exploding all around you, while you just have to move forward or become one of the casualties the planners had calculated, oh yes, before you hit the beach.

"But there was more for us to do.

"Going over, we had passed through the straights of Gibraltar and the sea was so rough we were all sick. We landed at night in Marseilles and they piled us into boxcars for freight and freighted us for a day before dropping us off less than a mile from where the Germans were. Soon enough, we fought. We fought a bloody path through the Siegfried Line, and it was no walk in the park. Pillboxes, anti-tank tracks, you name it. We found out the soldiers we'd killed in the end—mostly a lot of kids, you can't believe it, and old men. Before that, one guy who had bunked near me at Camp Gruber, a mortar hit near him and blew him way up into the air. When he came down screaming with fear it made all his hair fall out. Bald. And that was luck. We kept advancing. We crossed a river in rubber boats while they were firing machine guns at us, and more of my buddies "bought the farm" as they say, before they could get across. The river ran red.

"So Erin, we kept on going and the going was what it was, for the fewer of us. We all the same captured Wurzburg, Schweinfurt,

Furth, and Donauwort on the famous Blue Danube which is just a lot of poetry. It's brown and it stinks. Our planes did a job on these places and you can't believe what an ancient town looks like in rubble, as if it had exploded before it was ever finished becoming what it was; bits of intended loveliness were like forlorn orphans in the heaps of stone and plaster. But Mother Nature stubbornly keeps her agenda. Spring has come, our boots are dry, and we'd had Easter services with flowers blooming around us.

"Well, anyway the hospital here is spotless and very up-to-date. The Germans have excellent hospitals. We're in a handsome place that had been reserved for wounded German officers. Elsewhere in town, some 10,000 wounded, surrendered Kraut soldiers have been bivouacked, living as best they can, wherever they can, and dying.

"Garmisch didn't suffer an attack. The units from the crack mountain troops had surrendered it without a shot. It had finally sunk into their heads that the Reich was finished although for a while our people thought they were pulling a trick. Garmisch is by the way, a lovely city, with medieval streets. They paint buildings yellow in Bavaria. And the Alps with pristine snow are all around. Hard to pair the beauty of what still is intact in Bavaria with the evil that came out of here.

"We'd come to a place of unspeakable horror outside of Munich. It's hard to know how to begin. In the hospital here these doctors tell me to keep that whole event out of my thoughts. "I think that I'm scheduled to be sent to spend a little more time recuperating near Paris before I go home…"

Whatever wound he wouldn't mention, he was okay, and leaving all that behind in Paris…

♨

Near dawn, in my sleep, I had a nightmare: Water turned to fire. A river. I had been reading Homer for Literature class, and the dream must have evoked the Phlegethon. First it was fire, and then it was blood. My friend swimming across a river red with blood. The other side was fire again. And that burning shore somehow stayed with him all along, no elsewhere to reach by swimming faster. I was devastated by that image all next day. That evening, after supper, Jimmy telephoned…

After I hung up, I remembered Christmas, after the weeks of our mourning since the telegram.

Christmas morning he was at the door, devoid of the cheer of a wreath. He came with a gift for me, a novel by Henry James. My grandmother might have caught on that that difficult author was a tie between two keen-minded youngsters, as we sat with her, mostly silent—as if tiptoeing around my grief—drinking her thick hot chocolate. "The Spoils of Poynton." "A find," he called it. After he left, I saw his dedication on the flyleaf:

"For Erin, my oldest friend.

Jimmy King, December 25, 1941."

After that day, Jimmy was determined to take me under his wing again.

To the City. The first time we had gone there together, Manhattan was to me like going to another country with its rich civilization—the museums and luxury stores; where people who mattered and made the newspapers were living. I'd made that journey with my parents a few rare times. Tourists. The Christmas tree at Rockefeller Center. The Ringling Bros. Circus at Madison Square Garden. It had been a special treat, simple entertainment. With Jimmy—as soulmates—we were cultural immigrants. How should I look? That week I'd taken the braces off my teeth, thank goodness.

After that we would go to the City together on many weekends—to the museums, and even just to be there in the life of that richly sophisticated place. We would go through his copy of *The New Yorker* on the subway train.

Greenwich Village. With the charm of streets that made us think of what the revered look of Europe would be like. Bookstores with stands overflowing with old books. Cafés. There was a tall tree in Washington Square Park. "It's three hundred years old," Jimmy said. People were living there three hundred years ago. Jimmy had been here. He took us to a café he knew nearby called Caffè Reggio and we drank a frothy coffee called cappuccino.

We went to a bookstore with a dark scent among the shelves that I can still smell. Somehow that presence emanating from those old volumes took on a defining presence of importance; they defined things of the world that had to be told. Jimmy came back from a counter with something new: a leather-bound book of empty white pages.

"To be filled to the end, with the ambition you confided in me," he declared.

I was really moved that day. I was moved beyond saying thanks. He was, if you want to look at it that way, telling me that who I was and whom I would be could seriously matter in this world. Without a word. In that silence I could hear the quickened beating of my heart, while he held my wrist as his other hand handed me the gift.

Uptown, tall buildings loomed over the green acres of Central Park, with a startling congruity that brought to mind a special history of symbiosis—a metaphor of beneficent civilization. Once walking past the zoo, we paused to watch a man with a branch in his hand, his divining rod, looking for water. There was an allure that made his quest like magic a plausible thing in the exceptional life of the City.

Something inside me even told me that in another life this had been my home. And would be again.

We went one weekend to the matinee of a real play. We went Dutch on fifty-five-cent tickets, second best in the house. The *Times* had called it a "folk opera." The cast was all Black and they sang unforgettable songs: "Porgy and Bess."

Whoever were the girls star-struck by Jackson's star swimmer, whom Jimmy might have been also seeing, I did not know. Anyway, I couldn't see how that could change our complicity, and I saw no suitor whom I could class as worth being close with among the few dates I'd had in high school. I lost my shyness with him, like with a real sibling. Someone might have called our situation paradoxical: In that cerebral way we were more grown up, beyond the making out that was a compulsion among our peers growing up with the exfoliation of their sexuality. We had something rare and both felt elevated, in a sense, by what we saw as our shared way of seeing the world. And we were each, after all, the best student in our respective class.

That was the way we were then. How he was then...

Light filtered through the blinds. *My window*. His alarm clock showed seven now. The rain had diluted the heat. In the reality of the now Jimmy smelled bacon frying. He could hear the shower going in the bathroom next door, and his thoughts focused and became comfortably rational. It was Sunday, he knew, and his father was getting ready to preach today. The man's presence was part of the reality that comforted him. But it was a conflicted emotion.

His mind went back in memory. He was three years old...

August, 1929. On Jones Beach, an hour's drive further out on the Island, the year it was opened. And they'd walked, the three of them, along the vast, impeccable sand, past the impressive tower—a beacon, a lofty tribute by the state to the right all citizens had to a place of healthy leisure such as this. His father held him where the waves gave their last post-climactic babble, while his mother looked on in her dress, from the sand. When they came out of the water, with the sun quickly making the salt itch on Jimmy's skin, and with Jimmy's mouth dry, Pastor King held his son so that he could reach up to a water fountain on the brick walk. He turned a miniature ship's steering wheel to make the water spout. Jimmy steered; the wheel was big in his three-year old hands, as he imagined, with the water splashing in his face and his feet no longer grounded, high sea. Looking out at the ocean and the beige sand, Jimmy saw men in crisp, white sailor uniforms. They were keeping the sand immaculate, stabbing the few papers some people had left behind. Jones Beach. Jones's beach people in their part of Queens came to call it, always with a note of affection. As if Jones were one of their number sharing with them the enjoyment of his possession. An oasis of free Apollonian pleasure and health, at the edge of the ocean that stretched until it came to that feverish world on the other side. Someone had written somewhere that this beach that New York State had created was the most beautiful beach in the world.

Then they were taking an outdoor shower for washing off the sand and salt. He cringed under the cold water; his father drew him close and he felt his warmth. His mother, who never got past her shyness to wear a bathing suit, although her body was nothing to be ashamed of, stood by in that floral sundress, holding a towel and Jimmy's Buster Brown sandals.

He remembered that it wasn't just shyness that kept her from a bathing suit. Her sister had drowned from cramps off Virginia Beach, when the sisters were teenagers. She was fearful of the ocean, but she wouldn't let that fear inhibit her only child. When he became a champion swimmer, he thought of it always as retribution for her. But she could no help but grieve when she saw him off to war.

"Pass him to me. Don't put his feet down."

Keeping your child's feet free of sand was a problem for any mother in this world. The thought came to Jimmy with something like mirth...

Moe was scratching at Jimmy's bedroom door.

His father had finished his sunny side ups and bacon. He was sipping coffee and staring into space, going over his sermon in his mind.

"Did I hear you say yesterday that you're not going to church?"

"Yes, sir."

"Yes, you mean you're going?"

"No."

"Jimmy? You think it's appropriate that the pastor's son skips church?"

"I'm not skipping. I'm not going."

"What is that supposed to mean?"

Jimmy kept silent. His father turned red. He drank a swig of coffee as if it were a draught of medicine. The pastor fathomed what was going on with Jimmy. He'd dealt with doubt. He knew it well personally and fathomed it now in Jimmy.

"I knew what you knew," he said, "do you think the Woods were like Cunningham Park?"

"What I knew, my going to church isn't going to change that. If it would, I'd be your altar boy the rest of my life."

But now the pastor heard disrespect. He was the Marine again as he bolted up. His chair fell behind him. Moe, who'd been gnawing at a leather bone near the breakfast nook, began to protest loudly against what was going on in his family.

"You shouldn't talk to your father that way," Edith King said unassertively. As if she was, at the same time, diminishing its seriousness with an echo of a banal admonition to a child.

Jimmy was silent. Finally, he said with a gentleness which was like a glove over a clenched hand. He said what he couldn't hold back:

"You knew. Did you see children? You saw? Ovens. Bodies in ovens half-burned. Little bodies—

King held up his hand.

"You want me to stop?"

"Edith, I don't think you want to hear," King said.

He held up his hand until she left. Obediently.

"It wasn't on any battlefield," Jimmy said. His father reached across now the table to take his hand, as if he could make him stop, knowing that his son needed to stop. "Good Lord…" Jimmy said with a note of irony.

"Can we leave The Lord out of this conversation?"

"He's always there, isn't He? He's with you always, right, even when they're cutting you into pieces."

"I've been through it. And yes, I believe He was at my side."

"And the others?"

"What are we talking about?"

"All the others, Pop, whom He let scream until they died."

"Jimmy, I saw men being cut down all around me. I saw men…I don't want to go into all I saw at Belleau Wood."

"You know something, I knew worse. Bodies of innocent babies. They'd done horrible experiments on them, let them die of starvation and typhus. Parents, grandparents, children. And this place was a summer camp compared to the others—did you read where they gassed them all day long? Why, father, why did He have to do this?"

His father held back.

"I haven't got a good night's sleep ever since. Why do you think they put me in a hospital?"

"You've got to stop—"

"Stop what? Erase my brain. We came into the camp and the smell was enough to kill you. They were walking around like the living dead, like in some double feature horror movie. In these striped pajamas. Rain came down and they had nothing but those pajamas. They came up and kissed our hands, and for some it was with the last bit of strength they had in them. A mother handed me her baby to hold. The kid had a face all bitten by lice, and a blown-up belly. It wasn't even a kid anymore; it was something you'd never seen before. And this thing looked up at me and by the grace of God, you'd say, it smiled at me."

"You have to stop—"

"Stop what? Cut away this piece of my life? Can't do that. So I'm supposed to pray that it all could be reeled back—history could be reeled back—by the grace of God, and erased? And the kid would be playing with a teddy bear somewhere?"

Pastor King got up and turned his back.

"Look at me, Pop. He died while I held him. Give me the sermon!

"I went into this hangar, and there was nothing there but clothing. You see, not any of those skeletons who were walking around by the bodies piled up outside. Just clothing, for little kids. Shoes, sweaters—everything for little kids. Even their toys as well. Teddy bears. And they were sending all that stuff to the home front. Can you imagine giving your kid some dead kid's shoes? And how they died. They threw kids naked into pits with naked people and shot them and poured on lye, but some kids were treated differently. They had a doctor who tortured them with crazy experiments. We had a Jewish German GI interpret the witnesses. He got sick. Other guys got sick. They'd run off and throw up, but what was our sickness in comparison? Someone said they were throwing live kids right into the ovens. It was more efficient. They worked it out to save bullets that way—you could throw little kids into the oven—one, two, three—it wouldn't have been easy for grownups. And they said you could hear them screaming all through the camp.

"It was a place we captured. Outside Munich. No summer camp."

"I saw a newsreel," King said lowly.

"I held the kid with a belly like a balloon, too weak to cry until he died. You saw! You saw? You saw a nightmare that didn't need another address."

King hesitated until he answered. "It's better that you said all that you said."

"Better?"

"Better than living it over and over, Jimmy."

"Like the Catholics do in confession?"

"Maybe there is something like that there." King was fumbling for words now, with his indignation gone. Those last words evaded emotion, as their banality of expression brought a confirmation of the ordinary. He couldn't rely on that now. The register was out of place, and Jimmy wouldn't stop:

"The whole world has to confess for being part of the human race!"

The pastor was silent a long moment before he gave his own confession:

"The world is full of things, Jimmy, with all the whys we can never understand. We live by faith with incomplete knowledge. But the Lord gave us an understanding. He sent His Son to earth to help us to understand the difference between good and evil."

He looked at Jimmy to see if he'd understood that.

"To live by that."

Jimmy looked at him, becalmed, almost contrite. He said:

"Maybe such things are so awful that you have to black them out from memory—even from history. Like censored letters.

There's nothing to learn from them other than how much evil there is in our world. Nothing that contains a remedy."

The pastor couldn't manage an answer.

"I'm sorry Pop." The object of "sorry" wasn't expressed. If he could have, Jimmy might have said, "I'm sorry that I'm laying all my horror on you," but he didn't, and he was chastened looking at the bleak sorrowfulness on the pastor's face. He was sorry to taunt him, bringing up the inexplicable. But sorry that it existed and that Pastor King couldn't admit that he couldn't really explain why.

Jimmy couldn't turn away from his father's face. The realization came to him then, with remorse as he lowered his insistent look, that the pastor was much older than the one whose face he could see in his mind now, where he'd fled to memory again:

My eighth birthday...

Schwinn Bicycles had designed the Aerocycle, with the look of a fuel tank between the handle and the seat. It had a push-button bell that Jimmy would ring up and down the street. When he saw the bike model advertised in the *Long Island Press*, Jimmy learned that his father had actually spent thirty-five dollars on his bike.

It was in the summer that his parents had bought the house near Chestertown, upstate. The cabin. A little place on the lake. His summer house set the Reverend Dr. King above the means of his parishioners, but nothing could be called showy about it. It was, in fact, less comfortable than their house in Cambria. The "cabin" he called it. It was austere enough to have the feeling of camping. There was an outhouse instead of a toilet, which bothered Jimmy's mother to no end. King held that a runoff some day from an indoor toilet's septic tank on their little plot of ground might pollute the lake. But Edith had to deal, as well, with a kitchen sink served by a pump. In the end, that willful austerity when none was likely required was characteristic of the pastor. His moves were often motivated by abstract principles. The greatest abstract, of course, being the invisible One who made things what they are, with no easy way to reason beyond acceptance. His father could be very cold and that could torment Jimmy, but his cold principles were not wicked nor ever hypocritical. The son learned to ride the bike, and having learned to swim, Jimmy spent a lot of time in the lake. At night he'd be tired, and at the end of the season, King would light a fire in the fireplace in the sitting room and they'd listen to the radio together. Jack Benny always made his father laugh, except when he was doing his Jewish skits. He found them demeaning. He had no emotionally-charged animus toward other people's religious convictions—they were there with all else that was wrong in the world that you accepted as it was appropriately created, on faith. Which was not to say that he accepted the possibility that they might be on the exact same plane of truth and rightful worship as his own.

For the tangible things, Jimmy remembered his first swimming lessons with his father in the pulsing water of Jones Beach. He remembered his father's bringing Moe home as a gift inspired by his mother for his confirmation when he was eleven. Dr. King had spared Moe from being put down at the ASPCA's kennel of homeless dogs. Moe was homely, which would have kept others from adopting him. The pastor saw his bringing Moe home as a particular *mitzvah*, as his friend Rabbi Braun in the nearby Jewish neighborhood of Laurelton would call the blessing in saving the life of a creature, even an animal.

Jimmy came back to now and suddenly wasn't able to get another word out. King saw more grief in his son's face than he had ever seen. *Jimmy is sick.*

There was silence, until Edith came back in and saw them. She couldn't speak. She reached again, in the middle of their grief, toward a refuge in the normal, the simple, the everything right. She found a trivial gesture of concern, all she could say, as she refilled two coffee cups:

"Jimmy? How should I make your eggs?"

And then, with what might have risen up in him through an impulse of self-preservation, Jimmy's heart unbound itself and transported him safely to this world where you choose how you wanted your eggs. He looked at his mother. The look was patronizing. If he told her what it was like, she'd never believe him.

So Jimmy would have something in common with Dr. Cato Lyons. It was a time in history when what they had in common was indeed very common…

⚬⚬⚬

"Hellooo," Jimmy said.

He'd got back that voice on the telephone. It had almost shockingly that same bright, almost suaveness that was the way he used to sound: the varsity hero, the head of Arista, who'd taken distance from indulging in his celebrity at Jackson with an assurance that—beyond any need of boasting—gave him what could be called a benevolent tone. "Erin," he said, without a thought betraying his strange homecoming, "I've been dying to talk to you. I mean for so long." As if he'd been out of town. As if the nearly two years of our separation interspersed with his danger and fear were some willful equivalent of a few blackened sentences.

"Remember: I said that I'd ask you to your prom, and I— If you haven't promised some lucky guy in between—I want to renew my entreaty."

"I didn't forget," I said. "I wouldn't forget."

"That's a yes! And what about a movie?"

We were together all over again that afternoon. We took the Q4 bus to the Valencia in Jamaica. The Valencia was in another world from the humble, plain Cambria Theater on Linden Boulevard. It didn't matter what was playing to make going to the Valencia an event. Loewe's ads called it a "wonder theater," a crescendo of luxury just before the Crash. The wonder was sculpture and murals, wrought-iron rails, cherubs, half-shells in terra cotta, glazed tile pilasters, volutes, swags, gable. Stars shone in the ceiling before the film came on. If going to the movies had been seen during the Depression as an escape from life's desolations, the Valencia could give a thousand odd escapees a suggestion of paradise the moment they walked past the ushers in uniforms with gold braids on their shoulders and white gloves, to where, before the talkies came in, a huge Wonder Morton organ played near the screen. All that for the price of a movie ticket. A quarter of a dollar. Thirty-five cents in the orchestra. The specialness of the place lasted past the escapism of the Depression.

"The Clock" was on screen, with Judy Garland in her first dramatic role. The movie had created gossip. Luella Parsons, in the *New York Daily Mirror*, had pointed out that Judy Garland had the director Fred Zinnemann fired so that the man she was going to marry, Vincent Minnelli, could do the picture. In the film, her lover was Robert Walker, a soldier on a forty-eight-hour leave. He and Judy Garland fall in love and get married before he has to go off to the war. We didn't stay to find out how it ends.

A teenage couple was fiercely necking in the seats in front of us. We heard sucking noises.

"Let's go," Jimmy suddenly said. I was embarrassed as we made our way through our row of people. I had to apologize while he didn't. Outside the theater he looked confused.

It was still early.

"I don't really feel like going home. Let's walk," I said. I sensed that whatever moved him in the theater was something he had to walk off.

We walked for several blocks until the jumble of commerce on Jamaica Avenue gave way to the green expanse of a park. "Rufus King Mansion" the sign at the edge of the park read. We sat on a bench in this oasis.

"No relative," Jimmy said, for want of saying something else.

There was a moment of heavy silence.

"You know, there are two things I think that I have learned from the way my life has happened that I can do well," he said, "kill or swim.

"The choice is obvious. My goal is that I swim two years up at Cornell—they're taking me—and I hope to try out for the Olympics. And you?"

He waited for an answer.

"Seriously, you're still writing?"

He waited a decent time again for me to answer. I shrugged. He'd touched a sore.

I thought of the empty pages in the notebook he'd given me.

"Nothing to show anyone. I'll have a lot more to do at Barnard next year."

"You're happy to get out of Cambria?"

"There's a world out there. You've seen the worst of it, but you've seen it."

"The City, right? The City on the Hill" for people far across the river with brains.

He hesitated before he said:

"Incidentally. I don't trust my brain anymore." He tried to make it have the lightness of pointing out a matter of fact.

A softball rolled across the paved path while we walked. On the lawn near us, a group of about twelve boys were batting the ball around and catching it. Jimmy grabbed the ball and threw it straight and swift to the pitcher. They hadn't expected that. One kid clapped, so they all clapped. Jimmy's mood cued into their gesture and he clapped back.

Somehow, I sensed, he had come to the first moment of delight in our whole afternoon. I wasn't an athlete; I didn't feel how assuming gestures like that toss took you someplace good. Someplace else. All in all, since that moment in the movie theater, I felt we were elsewhere from the easy complicity we'd always felt. I felt solemn. We hadn't clicked. Something hadn't opened up. But Jimmy came back from the lawn with a new look of happiness. The athlete was who he was in that moment, as if in a phantom of his past.

"I'm renting the tux." He held out the shirt that hung on him with both hands. He laughed at his thin physique under it.

He let his hands fall and stopped laughing. *I am alive.*

He laughed again.

Then we laughed together. That day was the first time we were spending together in nearly two years. I reasoned that I'd heard him trying to bring his mind home in small talk.

THREE

The death of Dr. Alex Franklin, whom Cato Lyons would replace, had hit me very hard. My grandmother, who was Franklin's patient and beyond that a special friend, had put his benevolent presence into my life—to be his much-needed clerical assistant, on afternoons after school. It came to what I considered an opulent allowance, but more than that, the good doctor became a father figure for me, my real father being gone. If Jimmy seemed to me a surrogate brother, Franklin was that eminence, the need-driven other piece of my shattered family.

He named me "Miss Efficiency." It wasn't a trying job. The filing was easily done. Keeping his books took a little more time. He'd tell me who were among the people who owed him money whose debts were to be written off. He seemed to feel just happy with my presence, he who had no children of his own. It was more than needing someone to look after his papers. He could have called me his daughter figure.

Because the agenda of his consultations would last late through the evening, we never had the time to speak very much to each other. Once when there was nothing else for me to do, he came out of seeing a patient and saw me looking through his library. He said, "Take anything you want home to read."

He never asked me what I thought of all I read. Zola, Willa Cather…He had the insight, or the tact, to avoid taking on the competing role of a teacher like Sanford Rose who taught us his keen, studied perceptions in English class at Jackson. Dr. Franklin shrank from distilling in me what to think, while my thoughts could make their own original discoveries. He, himself, had never learned any critical doctrine to frame the way he read. He hoped that whoever would come to assign me reading would not lead me to wrong places, for the sake of some normal school learning. If judge were the word, he'd forever judge his reading by the counsel his grandmother had given him so long ago—bedtime stories from Grimm, in her reminiscent German syntax: "From stories we know what the world is."

Once, when it was his birthday, he took my grandmother and me to a ballet at the Met. My grandmother and her doctor had formed a devoted, mature, platonic friendship. His life had turned out to his being a bachelor. No one had that precise story. Iris Randall wasn't a widow. She'd been abandoned with a lot of bills by a pathological gambler. She'd never said a word about poor Terrence Randall other than about his addiction. She never mentioned him beyond that, not once. Franklin's remaining a bachelor might have been an unshaken grip on independence or privacy, whatever had provoked it. His ultimate generosity to Cato Lyons could be seen as a movement out of his self-awareness, his deliberate stroke of making touch with the world beyond it, like giving himself a place in the same tenements where he'd done house calls. Call it a shy, but profound empathy.

They carried out, Iris Randall and him, a kind of dance of etiquette in their refrains of intimacy that Henry James might have well depicted.

We attended "Fancy Free," choreographed by Jerome Robbins with a brilliant young conductor, Leonard Bernstein. Afterward, he treated his two women to beef Stroganoff and blinchikis, at the Russian Tea Room, where the headwaiter called him by his name. Franklin's treat wore the elegant gallantry that fitted his crushed linen suit and bow tie. I discovered that there was this bon vivant side of Dr. Franklin. When the waiter asked about cocktails, Dr. Franklin's face went serious. "It's my birthday," he said, and so he challenged his intimate enemies, his kidneys, with a Gibson, while my grandmother had a Rob Roy and I had ginger ale. He drank little sips, as if his drink was something too hot, and then he and my grandmother had a refill. I had never before seen her drink liquor except her crème de menthe, but she had worries enough to ease. Her daughter's war was still on.

My grandmother wiped the rim of her glass hard with her napkin before she drank. Franklin watched her with a lugubrious smile, and when she saw that she shrugged. That look of his seemed to be a combination of indulgence and maybe shame. It was an ineffectual gesture of hers, he knew, she knew, and anyway old people had little reason to be that cautious. But Franklin looked away quickly, as if Iris, with her reputation of directness, might have responded to his indulgent smile with the question: "What are you and your people doing about it?" She was capable of asking that, of that outspokenness. Her gesture might even have been a setup for that provocation.

The plague had not yet found a victim in Cambria, while people did such futile things in America that summer; they wiped away at glasses, washed harder, kept out of swimming pools. Children wore little bags of camphor around their necks on strings—

as if anyone knew that those things, or anything else, could protect them from the epidemic that came with the heat.

There was a moment of awkward silence, and then Dr. Franklin, on this birthday of which the recurrence of many more was subject to serious, professional doubt, went mellow, as if something tight he was wearing was unbound. Or those two Gibsons had negotiated with it for comfort.

He talked about himself and about the man who would keep his practice going. Already summing himself up? I had never allowed myself to be too curious about his life, but he was reaching to achieve a moment that would be something positive; he was telling things almost in the voice of a lesson. He spoke about Dr. Cato Lyons, who was going to take over. He felt "serene" about that. He could suggest the event of his dying, without saying it outright, as if he were telling them that he was planning to move house. Without even a touch of sadness. After two Gibsons. Bad kidneys—the doctor's own as well as those he treated—have no way of becoming good again.

He told how Cato's father had put them together, shortly before Lyons senior died. Cato was assigned to the Saint Albans Naval Hospital near Cambria for the last year of his hitch, no longer doing surgery, as he'd done in the field. When his father learned where it was, he told him that his old roommate, with whom he still exchanged Christmas cards, was a general practitioner very close by and they should get together.

Separated now from the wife who'd left him, Cato, he said, was living in three rooms in barracks beside the hospital. Every item in each room government issued, the epitome of comfort compared to what he'd known in the Pacific, but as decorative as a cell. Cato had told Franklin that the neighborhood "as best it could" compensated for his bleak quarters.

The hospital and the base were built on what had been an elegant golf course before the developers went broke with the Crash. Babe Ruth had liked to play there. Part of the course was also now a place called Addisleigh Park. He'd take walks among the sumptuous homes of Addisleigh, plantation manors with Greek columns, English country homes. "It's the most luxurious "ghetto in the world," he'd said. The list of famous colored people, all the great musicians and entertainers—Lena Horne, Count Basie— who lived there was long. Their fame notwithstanding, it was their golden ghetto, because both he and Franklin knew that few, if any, Whites anywhere were likely to sell a colored person a house in a White neighborhood. And when one actually did, all the neighbors would move away. Franklin's friend Cato had heard a story that Addisleigh became Black after a ruined stockbroker living there jumped out a window on Wall Street, and his wife had been desperate to sell…

Cato's father and Franklin had both studied pre-med at Northwestern. Lyons senior, Franklin revealed, didn't make the cut for any med school, and went on to study pharmacy. Alex, aided by the fact that his name was Franklin and not his father's original Fraenkel, escaped an unwritten quota on admitting Jewish applicants—the figure at Columbia Med was five that year—got accepted, and never went back west. Becoming a healer had been a genuine moral decision for him. A moral decision, but after Alex's internship at Bellevue and a few years carrying his leather case up and down the dusty stairways of the tenements of the Lower East Side, amongst the lung cases and the children with the growth problems of poverty, he gave in to the lure of absorbing less painful grief in Cambria Heights. He paid four thousand five hundred dollars for one of the almost identical little brick "Tudor" houses on 240th Street. He didn't say what brought him to that particular place, instead of buying into a practice somewhere else. My grandmother told me that it seemed another moral choice, or a moral compensation for his giving up on The Lower East side: to join in and serve America's faith in its future, during the heart of the Depression, among people who, in those dark times, had managed to raise themselves from being poor to lower middle class. All that might well have been a rationalization. The Lower East Side—not to mention the emergency ward of Bellevue—had been Franklin's version of a war story, in which he found a way to survive. He apparently hadn't enough money, in any case, to buy into a fancy practice and med school may have taught him that he hadn't the rarer mettle of a specialist. He had found his level and now his place. He went out to this new community, where there was no doctor closer than Jamaica, and attached himself to the life of the place. He was a bachelor who may never had known intimacy, a listener, and a healer to a host of people. A good, kind, reasonable man, the best foil as a friend for Cato Lyons.

He made him his heir, judging, from all he knew of him, that he was, in important ways, indeed his natural heir.

The last time that I saw Dr. Franklin, I'd come to the hospital. Near the bed where he sat propped with a look he'd screwed up of pleasure, he pointed to the black box on a table near him.

"That's for you, Erin," he said. "Mary has brought it here for you to take home." It was the portable Smith Corona from his office. In all my time as his part-time girl Friday, I'd never seen him use it. For some reason, doctors always write out their prescriptions with a handwriting only they and pharmacists can read, some ancient practice within their symbiotic fraternities. But the typewriter had a place alone on a table close to his desk. Maybe some poor writer, who'd at last sold a book well, had given it as token of gratitude for the many free consultations that had saved him to write that book. Keeping Franklin's records, I knew that people were having trouble paying him. He might have found a use for that typewriter out of its case as a kind of ornament, but I came to see, in that presence close to him where he spent long days, a little monument to what he revered. In his living room next door, his library stretched from wall to wall and up to the ceiling.

Franklin wanted to give the machine to me personally. When I got home and opened the case, there were war bonds made out in my name under the Smith Corona. Whatever he'd intuited, like a fine diagnostician, was expressed in his note: "You'll know what to do with this." The occasion had made those parting words resonate with solemnity, giving them, as he'd meant them, the imperative force of an important prescription.

He died the next day. To Mary his housekeeper, whose husband was partly crippled, he left his immaculate, bought-used '33 La Salle and a sum of money as well.

Cato Lyons would be the last one to see him alive. He crossed Iris in the hospital hallway, going to his room. I never knew what last minute confidences might have been passed on between the two healers...

The time come, I would take the Smith Corona to college and make it my inanimate companion, with me even now though it's silent and I have gone on to what is called a word processor. It was as if, and probably indeed so, that Dr. Franklin intuited it as a key to my future. Although he wouldn't be there to know it.

Neither would Dr. Lyons...

చ్ఛు

The Reverend Dr. King wasn't ever happy about Jimmy's being with me, since we'd grown up. He knew that Catholics marrying a person not of their faith would expect that person to convert. He'd taken into account the risk of such a marriage and seeing his son become a "someone worshipping according to a Pope," even if it was pretty clear that we were not "going steady." Truth to tell, I already had my doubts about worshipping, and I hadn't regularly gone to confession since my father was killed. I have since been, truth to tell, an off and on hopeful agnostic, but I can't rationalize the hope. I sometimes think that, if I were an ancient Roman, I'd have believed in the existence of Fortuna, the Goddess of the luck of the draw, but I couldn't call that a devotion.

Before Jimmy had phoned again, he had, in any case, had a talk with his father; the upshot was that the Reverend Dr. King had lent him the Packard. It was a seminal moment. Dr. King, who wasn't a man out of touch with reality, conceded that Jimmy, home from the War, wasn't a kid now, and all he could with any dignity do was to advise. Jimmy told him that we were going to be three couples on a beach party. He knew the other boys; they worshipped at his church. Jimmy needed a car and his father reached out his affection and lent him the Packard.

I packed a two-piece bathing suit and a towel, and Jimmy drove his father's Packard to Jones Beach.

We didn't pick anybody up. Jimmy said, "Actually, I thought it would be nice if it was just us. I've been having trouble connecting with old connections." Looking back, what should I have thought? There were a lot of other cars in the parking lot at the beach. Beach parties under the stars at Jones Beach were a common thing. We found a quiet corner, behind a low, grassy dune. The sun was setting and its low rays were sparkling on the waves until they ended in foam on the sand. Jimmy had brought a khaki army blanket.

"A souvenir," Jimmy said, "it kept me from freezing."

Tonight there was no chance of freezing. It was a beautiful summer evening, the sky just black and glittering with stars, a faint breeze coming off the ocean smelling of brine. Fireflies blinked. We were comfortably far from anyone.

Jimmy had a bottle of wine. He went to the shore, scooped up sea water, and placed the bottle of rosé wine from France in his pail. I think, if I remember right, that I had never tasted wine before, except for Communion. He'd been through France.

I changed, wrapping my towel around me, while Jimmy peeled off his pants down to his swimsuit, and we ran into the water.

We drank several paper cups full of the wine, while he reclined close to me on the blanket. It was chilly after the swim, and his warmth near me was a comfort. I looked at the panorama of stars in the sky until I turned his way and saw that his eyes were closed. By his breathing, I could tell that he'd actually dozed off. His breathing got heavier, and then suddenly he jumped up. Before I could make a sound, he was rushing away on the beach. The wind rose, and that and what had just happened made me tremble. I sat there alone and nervous while he was gone in the dark. I felt pretty strange, wondering if I should have come here, thinking about the other two couples who were supposed to be with us. I wondered how long it would be before we headed home.

I startled when he came up behind me and put his hands on my shoulders. His lips grazed the back of my neck, and when I turned, he kissed my mouth. Gently, different from the wild reactions that he'd gone through. I kissed back. I can still say that it wasn't passion then that moved me. It was maybe as much a way I answered what had been his pain. With all the fear I felt about this situation, my heart went spontaneously out to him.

Then it happened.

We were suddenly connected physically, but the easy, warm closeness we'd known as friends was at the same time gone—we were paradoxically distanced from each other, from whom we'd been; I felt the painful closeness as an interloping thing, an intrusion rather than a bonding. It was over quickly.

I had let it happen.

Somewhere someone was playing music on a harmonica. A radio came on and I heard the sound of swing at the "Make Believe Ballroom."

The music faded. We didn't talk. For a long time...

I'd crossed over to a different me, and I was left, exhausted, with the sense of having accomplished a passage, not ecstatic, but as exciting as fear. Vague fear, and then remorse. And what did I finally feel I had lost? Not what comes first to mind—the passage to womanhood. Dignity. Finally, it felt low. After all the high thoughts that were our history.

He spoke. Not about what we had just done. "I used to hear that music. Dorsey," he said, "the Germans played it to us. Axis Annie. And she'd play jazz and mock us for our Negro music."

He was back there again.

I didn't know what to say. Neither of us would speak about the change in who we were. He kissed me again, awkwardly. I sensed a tinge of apology. The change indeed frightened me now. We were bound together in a deeper, more consequential way than we'd been. For the worse?

He spoke, taking us elsewhere, to emotionless conversation. "It's great about Barnard. You're going to live in the City?'"

"It's provided in the scholarship."

"The City. That will be great."

"Great," I said.

We were making small talk.

He sent out a feeler of emotion.

"I'll be far away," he said, "High again above Cayuga's waters."

Cornell. Where he'd be. And I'd be elsewhere. I was confused. Like the coming together, would anything be consequential in the separation? Were we, in a way, forcibly attached now?

We got home very late. I can't remember what we said on the way home, if we indeed said anything at all. Once, when the reflection of a traffic light revealed his face, I saw such anguish that I wanted to reach out and relieve that somehow. I took his hand.

When we reached 240th Street, everyone seemed asleep. No radios going. Darkened houses.

Jimmy drove up to my house, and we kissed before I got out. It was as if each of us felt we were doing what we were supposed to do now. We didn't say anything about where we were going next, not even when we'd see each other next.

I stood at the door, confused, until Jimmy went inside his. My grandmother was doing a crossword puzzle, waiting up for me, when I came in. She looked up, perturbed, as I headed straight for a shower.

"A shower?" she said.

"Sand."

I let the shower run for a long time. There was sand in the

drain when I got out, which gave me the perverse thought that I hadn't lied to my grandmother. She'd gone to bed, and I went up to my room, my place, the attic that my father had converted to a large private place.

My place. I lay on my bed, looking up at the pine rafters that my father, good with his hands, had put up. I thought of him. What would he think of me now? Our photo with me between Mom and him was on my night table. A big picture of him in his sailor suit, white hat with his pompadour touching the rim, those bellowing pants, the neckerchief. That picture on the wall, the uniform, was like a document of proof that he'd become someone else, the someone else he'd chosen. Fatefully...

I turned on the radio. He'd bought it for me, my own radio in my own place. Bright canary yellow Bakelite. "Because you're so bright," he'd joked. I had it tuned, as always, to the same station. It was too late for the "Make Believe Ballroom" and "Your Hit Parade," but there was some disc jockey out there in the night. He spun The Ink Spots:

To Each His Own.

My father. He was mine and I was his and we four, with Grandma were each other's. The nucleus of my world, of my life, until the day the Western Union man came, and it was violently sundered. My place. My rag doll collection hanging out of my bookcase with my collection of books going back to children's stories. All this too was me. Could I, in a sense, have betrayed that self and that intimacy, with this new unclear other?

I lay awake a long time before I fell asleep...

⁓

Jimmy's father was awake when he arrived home. He was drinking tea at the kitchen table, when Jimmy came in the side door of the house and saw him in his bathrobe. He was sitting there with a calendar making notes on his kids' softball schedule for the summer.

They had words.

"It's late," his father began, "did you notice the time?"

"Pop, I'm a grown man. Please don't talk to me like a kid."

"You're my son, and always will be. I can tell you what's right. If I can't tell my son what's right, what can I tell my parishioners?"

"What's wrong?"

"I don't like what's going on."

"Going on?"

"What you're doing running around with the Burke girl."

"Running around?"

"Or whatever worse."

Jimmy didn't answer that.

"She's Catholic. I have nothing against Catholics. I just don't wish my grandchildren to leave my faith."

"Who's talking about grandchildren?"

"What else do you have in mind? Fooling around?"

"Fooling around? Fooling around? Geez—"

"Can we leave profanity out of this conversation?"

Pastor King got up and turned his back.

"Go ahead. Give me the sermon!"

Upstairs, Edith woke to his shouting. She buried her head under her pillow.

His father stared out the kitchen window at the night.

They were silent for a long time. Jimmy finally got up from the table and put his arm around his father. He wanted to let him know that nothing was his fault, that he was a good man. That all that had bound them together for years was something that should never be severed. The bond. Love. And all at once he had the sinking feeling that, like a flash of mica in a pool of water, he'd sensed a fragment—a fragment of the ties he'd thought he'd come back to whole and that were now in turgid confusion.

He turned and left his father at the window. The pastor's heart reached out to him as he kept walking, stooped, stiff—as if maimed. Changed—maimed—without even a good-night. Jimmy went up to bed and buried his face under the strange sheets.

It was as if we could believe that the whole thing never happened, or rather that what had meant much to us, our rare togetherness, could continue across the crucial event with shared remorse, and that shared remorse confirmed our attachment. We wanted it back, or so I felt that Jimmy did, in all his unreasoned confusion. I was, I couldn't help it, full of a confusion of emotions, none of which even reached me with decisive clarity. It was the first time that we were together since that night at Jones Beach. And that in its dominate eventfulness, kept its hold on my mind. Without even being quite conscious of what I was doing, I let two IND trains go by without the courage to face up to the all-engrossing question of what next.

So we had arranged to meet in the City after each of us would have accomplished a worthy mission elsewhere from our predicament. He was going to buy a gift for his father's fiftieth birthday. It was the day that I went up to Barnard to sign for my housing. My roommate, I learned, would be a girl from England, and I looked forward to that touch of cosmopolitanism in my life, although I wondered how the style-less beds, desks, and chairs would match her expectation of luxury that had been spared a war. It would be the trappings of another chapter in my coming of age, in any case, just a short distance, geographically, from the previous one.

Jimmy and I had left from home at different times but we'd arranged to have lunch together. Jimmy said we'd meet outside the Automat in Times Square.

We left the blare there of Times Square, the traffic stuffed with yellow cabs and the huge signs that were giant exhortations to consume. A big face was blowing smoke rings through a hole in a wall. I saw the New York Times building and remembered when I had seen, in a newsreel, the motionless crowd with drawn faces, looking up at the ticker unreeling war. Now nobody in the undulating crowds seemed to be excited about anything. The anxiety had been replaced by less consequential resignation. I felt an insignificance in the movement of the crowds, where people walked and wove among them, stopped to eat hotdogs, or to go on to destinations equally ordinary, while on several street corners men were foisting flyers with various small appeals to disposable income.

We pushed through the revolving doors of the Automat, and it seemed a sudden oasis from all of that. The whole room seemed to take on a different, more alluring light. As if a message in the gleam of all the chromium of a bright future. Jimmy's face brightened as soon as we found a table close to the wall of food slots. When we sat down, Jimmy showed me the gift he'd bought from the vintage watch dealer among the jewelers of 47th Street. It was a Cartier from 1929, in the "tank" style that Louis Cartier had designed in 1922 for General Pershing, vaguely resembling in shape the view of a World War One tank seen from the air. Rare. He had the whole story from the dealer, Mr. Millikian, before parting with a good portion of his accrued army pay. Jimmy was onto war again, but it came to me that he was going out of his way to honor—to flatter—his father. The Reverend Dr. King, retired Captain King, had repaired and re-repaired the "wristlet" that had been on his wrist in battle. It was a round pocket watch with lugs welded on it to take a strap, worn by soldiers before wristwatches came into style. It hadn't even had a maker's name on it, but it had endured, as he had, although the wristlet had nearly caused him to be late to preach to his parishioners more than once. The gift that would replace it was special. Jimmy was pleased by my opinion. I wouldn't ask him what he'd paid. He was up in a few seconds, off to the cashier, and came back with two fistfuls of nickels.

I remember his mood that day. He was trying to connect to happiness. Happy with the thought of getting closer again with his father. But it was the Automat that unbound his euphoria. It seemed to light him up.

I looked around, while he threw his nickels into the slots behind which hidden people were feeding them, pledged to keep the illusion of their non-existence. I'd asked for an egg salad sandwich on rye. I wasn't hungry and maybe I should have got up and sought out something more exotic. Jimmy returned with three sandwiches equally banal. But he had a look that made it seem that they were, for him, bounty that came with the pleasure, I sensed, of opening those slots. He got us coffee, and stopped to watch, staring like a child at the mouths of chromed lions while they poured.

The place gave off a strong feeling, but it wasn't fright over an eerie robotic, dehumanized setting. It was as if a universal force— for which we needed no understanding nor the anguish of seeking understanding—caused this manna to be. You cashed your money for nickels, and benevolently inexpensive coffee poured from the mouths of gleaming lions; clean windows clicked open with food precisely the same each time.

I thought of "A Clean Well-Lighted Place," the story by the author of a stricken generation that Sanford Rose had us read in English class: a pitiful, illusory shelter from the world's rain of calamity. The aura of the Automat had with it an illusion of succor. And Jimmy seemed to have touched base there, and had profoundly found succor in the illusory. The Automat was a small but resonant furlough from the life outside. History disinfected.

I don't remember what we said to each other. I think that it was next to nothing, but I believe that we both were touched again by a frail spark of the goodness of being together. The big place was nearly empty of other people; lunch hour was over, thanks to my delayed subway ride. The citizens had gone off to their stations of toil.

It was, though, looking now with clarity, really three worlds come together incongruously there: the jumble that had become his, mine, and the place he assumed that was only, ultimately, a stage performance sample of a science fiction world. But it might have indeed meant for him—with its stark strangeness, its chrome unreality—the escape from the ordeals of elsewhere as in a beyul. It was, as he once told me about Buddhism, the place where the endured world becomes, in a way, blotted of presence, with the peace of spirituality.

All in all, we were in exile, both us, on this trip that brought us nowhere together far enough from that fateful moment on a beach.

While we rode the subway back home, he nearly didn't speak. He seemed, for then, to be still in the moment of the Automat.

For Jimmy, compared to his hole in the ground, where you did not know if and when a mortar would land and kill you, the Automat was an embodiment of The Good Place, exquisitely predictable and promising: You threw in your nickels and dimes and the good arrived.

All in all, the place was fake. He would still be in distress for the good to arrive again in his life…

FOUR

On May 30, 1946, that day when Dr. Lyons arrived in Cambria Heights, he made the mistake of driving his 1939 Hudson Custom Eight by way of Linden Boulevard, and got as far as 219th street before he was blocked by the parade. His memories being in the state they were, he'd rather not have been there for this, but he had no choice when a patrolman made him pull over and park in front of the Cambria Movie Theater. The pause brought on an old reflex: He reached into his glove compartment for a treacherous former friend, then remembered that it wasn't there and, if his will held, it need not be there again. He took a Lucky Strike still in its white wartime package, lit it with his battered Zippo, inhaled deeply, and got out and stretched his long legs. As he left his car, he put on his seersucker jacket over his sweaty shirt, to assume the decorum that came with a doctor's obligation always to inspire trust through dignity.

His head towered above the others on the crowded sidewalk. William Cato Lyons was six-feet-six inches tall, a height that had proved to be an advantage when he'd been Princeton's center fielder before the War, but had been a hindrance when he'd been performing operations as quickly as he could in the tents. His seersucker suit, custom-tailored to his size by a Chinese tailor in Honolulu, hung loosely on him because of the weight he'd lost since then. At thirty-seven, he looked more than a decade older. Gaunt. Some epicures of observation might say attractively gaunt, as suffering sometimes redeems the physical loss of comeliness with character. His frame had grown wiry from physical stress, his face weathered by much sun. His jet-black eyes were a marker, with his sharp nose, of what his father William Pliny Lyons considered were his great-grandmother's Sioux genes, which had mingled with those of a Welsh settler who'd crossed The Great Divide, on a wagon train of fervent optimists.

The Welshman's wagon had been drawn by cows that gave his child milk, when his wife had died—wasting away of what could not be diagnosed other than starvation—before they'd reached the plains. The son survived and he brought him with him to his second marriage to a part Indian woman less comely. They raised their new family where—going from farmers to merchant townsfolk in the town that went up—the ancestral sacrifices paid off in a generation: The Lyons prospered modestly.

He was somewhere far away from fulfillment now in his own life. With those thoughts, he put a seal on memory.

The parade passed. Children came first. Brownies, wearing beanies with their brown dresses and gold-colored scarves. The stoutest among them were at the head, straining to hold high their troop's banner and Old Glory, while at the end of their number, four girls abreast wore sashes that read "Onward Christian Soldiers" and another row held up the colors of their Methodist Church. Right behind, was another troop of Brownies whose banner read "Sacred Heart" led by an elderly priest in black.

Girl scouts and Boy Scouts followed, and then there were real soldiers. Recent veterans in uniforms, some already too tight now. Soldiers, marines, sailors, airmen. WAVES, WACS. The Fife and Drum Corps of the VFW Post 123 marched after them, playing alternately with a brass band of the American Legion. He heard the notes of the "Halls of Montezuma" and "Off We Go into the Wide Blue Yonder," the hymn of the Army Air Force. Middle-aged men passed more slowly wearing puttees and the rough woolen uniforms of the American Expeditionary Force of 1917. The gray-haired Pastor King walked among them, marching with the authentic, remembered bearing of a Marine. Then there were two wheelchairs pushed by two Boy Scouts. Wrinkled men sat in them beaming vacantly. They wore no uniforms, not shoes but felt slippers; their sashes said that they were Rough Riders.

Women in plain dress were the last to pass. No flags, no banners, just the felt rectangles that had been hanging in their windows, in a pattern of red, white, and blue, that the women held solemnly. On each was the gold star that honored a fallen beloved. He saw grief and bitterness on their faces that pride before a public crowd could not erase.

Lyons watched it all pass and dissolve down the long boulevard, with a lack of emotion that surprised him, and ultimately comforted him. Before a chain of neurons could carry over into a burst of violent memory, someone tapped his arm. It was the Catholic priest who had been in the parade.

"Doctor William Lyons? Ignore me, if I guessed wrong. I saw the MD on your license plate, and you look like what Alex Franklin said you'd look like. You're our new Alex." His eyes measured Lyons from tip to toe, as if the exceptional physique before him was the confirmation, like an answered password: The genuine Lyons whom Franklin had described had arrived.

The man who spoke had the craggy mien of Pat O'Brien who portrayed a lot of priests in the movies. He was in his costume: a black suit with a priest's collar and a black fedora. And black gloves in the summer—a priest's odd, surprising dandyism?

"I'm the humble replacement."

"Well welcome to Cambria, sir. And he said you played checkers."

"Yes, we did."

"I'm Father Gerald Maloney. There are people who get away with calling me Gerry. I'm really not bothered by that."

"Cato."

"Excuse me, it isn't William. Have lunch with me, Doctor, unless you've already been invited to a barbecue."

Cato wasn't listening for a moment. It had just come back to him that some of the children in the parade were wearing little white sachets like tea bags hung around their necks. Camphor. Summer had arrived full of leaves and flowers, and threatening to become again the grim reaper in a seductive disguise. He didn't believe in the preventive power of the effluvia of camphor. But what else worked?

"That's very kind. I'd like to."

Gerry Maloney, D.D. led Cato Lyons, M.D. to the Canton Palace, just up the street from where Lyons left his car.

They took a booth near where a fan was turning and nodding back and forth adding to the coolness of the darkened, long dining room. Mr. Liu brought an aluminum pot of dark tea with the menus. One from Group A and one from Group B were the choices of the twenty-five-cent luncheon.

Both their wonton soups came out steaming. Father Maloney blew on his, holding his bowl as carefully as he had the habit of holding a chalice—as if there was the something of respect in the gesture.

"They say you cool off when you drink hot in hot weather," he said. "The body is the soul's mysterious companion."

Liu came up to them with spare ribs and egg rolls for them to share. "Everybody is at a barbecue," Liu said. "Have some, no charge."

They followed his resigned look as he took in the long empty dining room. They could see, at the far end, two men—the only other diners.

Maloney stayed with the egg rolls, while Lyons ate the spare ribs eagerly with his hands.

"It all ends with delightful barbecues," Maloney said.

Cato asked, "Will it all really end? What do you make of Potsdam?"

Maloney's face gave an expression of impotent uncertainty.

"You were in the Pacific, Alex told me," he finally said.

He took Cato's lack of a reply as an assent.

"I was at Bataan the second time," the priest said.

"Tarawa…and elsewhere." Cato said.

"Hell on earth, Doctor."

"Everywhere out there. Name the place."

The priest looked down the dining room.

"That's Jimmy King, Pastor King's son come home, back

there," he said. "I never saw the colored fellow before."

He raised his eyebrows to express the phenomenon: A Black stranger eating lunch with the local war hero. But he had on an Ike jacket, too, with civilian pants.

"A colored person in a restaurant in Cambria is an exceptional presence," he said, "but he should eat wherever he wants. This isn't Mississippi."

Cato had no reason to believe that Maloney might have said that for his conscience's sake. For him, humans were humans. He knew the likeness of all their vulnerable bodies, and he'd devoted his life to caring for and saving them from being nothing.

Maloney shifted to: "Excuse me, if you're a Catholic, Doctor, I'd be very pleased if you joined us at Sacred Heart."

"Am I a Catholic? My father converted us to it. He was sick and he was cured against all the doctors predicted. He made his extreme, grateful commitment to God. I have to say, I'm a lapsed Catholic."

Maloney nodded thoughtfully.

"You can understand, maybe, why?"

"Well, I'm not an evangelist, Doctor. Faith comes when it comes without a recruiting officer."

They drank their tea.

The strong dark tea had a salutary punch and brought with each a fragile note of euphoria. The priest looked quickly at Cato a moment, as if asking to hear more about his Pacific. But Cato just sipped his tea, and they both went on to eat their chow mein with appetite in the silence that Gerry—the word is honored—intuiting it as a mental version of a large bandage not to be removed.

Cato took notice of Maloney's eating with his gloves on.

From down the room, James King Jr. and his Black lunch companion walked past their booth toward the cash register. Jimmy gave a quick nod of recognition to Father Maloney, while the other man, in his Ike jacket, limped ahead.

꽃

Cato pointed the Hudson into the driveway on 240th Street, and it glided smoothly up to the garage like a horse that knew the way. Getting out of the car, he brushed against the hedges that separated Alex's driveway from the backyard of his neighbor, whose name, Cato remembered, was Gustav Loburg. Cato heard in his mind, Alex Franklin's nickname for his neighbor: Herman the German. Alex Franklin, at one time Fraenkel, had his own roots reaching back to Germany, but they'd been cut ragged.

Cato got his valises from the trunk and took out his inherited key. When he got to the side door of the house, he found it open, and the screen door was unlocked. Inside, the house still smelled faintly of the smoke from Alex's pipe. London Dock, a smell more like the smell of an oriental joss stick than of burning tobacco. Dr. Franklin, he thought, a subtle diagnostician and a delicate healer, had always favored the gentle over the strong. "Home," Cato heard a voice in him say, with the faint tone of a question and without the emotion of relief that people have when they hear themselves say "home." He was tired. Too much jumbling around in his mind. The newness of "home" made it all unbalanced, with something on a spectrum of emotion like fear. He closed his eyes and sat down on the seat of a stuffed chair that had worn into the shape of a dead man. And then "death" and "smell" brought him uncontrollably elsewhere.

Rotting flesh. He stepped outside the tent to breathe and his nostrils caught, like a knife blow to his own flesh, the stinking smoke of limbs burning in a barrel. A swarm of mosquitoes attacked his face and with that he reheard what a nerve case was saying: "We were waiting for them to attack. First, night after night they came with no noise—like ghosts. Right through our perimeter and then they start banging. They're banging, banging. Like they've come with pots and pans instead of guns, and then—they're gone. Ghosts. Guys with cut throats left behind... believe it."

Psychological warfare. Big word, little people, desperate, fanatical and doomed. Tarawa.

Now like a reprieve, he heard someone upstairs singing calypso sweetly, sweetly with a lisp, and that must be Alex's Mary.

Women, she sang, were smarter than a man in every way. It brought on a nagging personal fact check...

Cato had heard that sweetly syncopated voice before, but couldn't place the moment, among those he'd spent together with Franklin and talked a lot...

Alex wouldn't play the counselor, the ad hoc analyst, even though he knew well enough that Cato was not in good shape.

Nerves. He chose just to be there, to make this place nothing more than a sort of R&R for Cato's inner turmoil. The two doctors of medicine would go on about movies, or about baseball. DiMaggio was back that year from the Army Air Force. Some informed sportswriter broke the unconfirmed report that Branch Rickey, president of the Brooklyn Dodgers had signed up a Negro player he was grooming to break the color barrier on the Dodger team.

When Cato would arrive late, it was a time for Alex to get out of the office—where he spent long days—and they'd hang out in the kitchen, bypassing the waiting room that Alex had furnished with banal stuffed, false leather chairs from Gertz's department store in Jamaica. It looked empty of patients—bleak, as if invisible currents of distress lingered on in the air and endowed the place its pathetic mien. They sat instead at the Formica kitchen table. Alex would load his percolator with coffee, freshly ground at Bohack's supermarket on Linden Boulevard. It was a notch above other coffee. "My Miss Efficiency, who comes in part time taught me the art," Franklin would say.

Coffee was what they had.

Cato had said hastily that he didn't drink, before Alex might suggest alcohol. With that, Alex perceived that Cato was setting forth an immediate message against temptation.

Alex said that his own health didn't permit alcohol, without suggesting he'd sensed Cato's problem, but he could not help but perceive, after their many evenings together, what the demons were that were responsible for it. He himself had been too old to go over, and Cato had perceived a stubborn—albeit unjustified—guilt on the old doctor's part, whenever he'd—rarely—let the conversation drift toward the War. There were his relatives over there. Were…

Cato and Alex would play checkers after the reheated good dinners that Mary would leave, and drink coffee into the night. And their talk had stayed away from what had to be stayed away from. Franklin's goodness was joined by tact. Cato's affection for his father's old friend grew out of that. Alex never offered him more, until the generosity of his last testament.

With talk about sports and movies, they'd go on to books. Or music. They shared a risk of self-deprecation in being insensitive to the thrills of Wagner and also their distaste for him as a human being. They both thought that Steinbeck had heart. But they agreed that he didn't have the demonic drive—the *duende* as Cato put it—of Faulkner. They agreed as well on the talent of Joe DiMaggio.

There was little shop talk after Franklin's long day of intimacy with a string of ailments—just enough for Franklin to perceive that Cato would be a humane, sympathetic, and knowledgeable family doctor, before he decided on his gift. Cato had let him know that he no longer "felt right" after the emergency surgery he'd done, and Alex thought he'd once seen Cato's hand tremble over the checker board. Cato, in any case, had gone into the service before he'd established a practice to go back to.

A bachelor with little money and no living relatives, Alex passed onto Cato a prolongation of his own calling, and he must not even have been certain that it was a beneficent gift, although he knew keenly Cato's need for a change and an anchor to send down. He willed him his practice with his house to make what he would make of it, without yet knowing whether Cato was in the right mind to accept that.

So that was Cato's luck of the draw when it came to a mentor: a paragon of both generosity and humaneness.

And here Cato was. With nowhere else to go…

৵

"Mary?" Cato called. He heard a motor.

She had stopped singing and was in the bedroom, vacuuming.

She stopped to offer her hand when he came in. It was a gesture he wouldn't have expected from a colored maid. He held it a moment, getting acquainted again with this presence in his new life.

"Dr. Franklin said that you'd need me," she said. Her voice dropped. "It was one of the last things he told me."

"Yes…he was right. I'm glad, Mary."

"I come five times a week. The Siegals don't need me more than once, they said."

Mary was the West Indian maid whom Louis "Lepke" Buchalter had assigned to the Siegals—his in-laws—who, unused to servants, passed her on to Alex for all but a day a week. Lepke had also given his in-laws his Collie, Trixie. Lepke was very fond of Trixie, but he couldn't be with her while he stayed in hiding at some undisclosed other place, with a $50,000 reward for his capture.

"Doctor," he heard Mary say behind his back, "is it going to be another terrible summer for the sickness?"

He didn't answer. How should he be expected to know? No one knew what made the sickness come and go. And worse than that, no one really knew what to do about it. Asking a doctor was like asking a priest a favor from God.

The thought came to him that Mary was paradoxically lucky. In Harlem, where she lived, for some unexplained reason, the rate of polio infection was far below that of nice white neighborhoods. For some reason, luck again, perhaps, a case of polio had not turned up in Cambria Heights so far that year...

Cato spent a restless night in his new bed; it was a choice between staying awake or risking nightmares. He tried at least to relax his limbs totally each at a time, clinging to the straw of a belief that had never proved itself to him that this would give him some of the refreshment of sleep. Sometime after sunrise, he heard the thwack of the newspaper on his front door screen. Face the day.

When he stepped onto the lawn to get the paper, re-entering the world, he suddenly heard girls giggling. Staring at him were four teenage girls in light skirts, bobby socks, and saddle shoes, each of them cradling books. The school year was winding down, maybe that explained their gaiety; their voices projected haste, excitement. Giggles. Cato realized that of course nothing explained that laughter more than his being there in his shaggy bathrobe, red-eyed, and unshaven. Not a way for a doctor to appear. He leaned down to pick up the *Long Island Daily Press* from under his azalea bushes—Alex's subscription was still running, although a past edition had published his obituary. Cato unfolded the paper. Once far away in time now, he too had delivered newspapers on his bike. He knew the fold—the last rap you give it that blocks the tucked paper from opening when you toss it. The *Des Moines Register*. At a time made very remote by the crowd of things that happened to him since. The exciting news then was always the bootlegger raids. The boy's toss onto the lawn, this morning, was the kind of error he used to hate to make.

Cato looked again at the teenagers disappearing down the street. One of them, a red-haired girl with a long ponytail, saw him again as they turned the corner. He was reaching for the pack of cigarettes that he'd left in his bathrobe the night before, when he'd sat in Alex's Barcalounger reading, a bestseller, "The Razor's Edge." He realized that unless he could junk the cigarettes as well as the whisky, the house and the office would soon smell far less agreeably than of aromatic pipe tobacco. Remembering the Barcalounger, designed as a place in which to settle old bones comfortably, Cato was struck by a regret that he had short-circuited his life or been short-circuited by it—both actually—by being here. The question was: What else could he do or where else could he be? And he allowed himself the thought that Alex had made him a gift of honorable responsibility. A definite calling...

⚜

I was that red-headed girl with a pony tail.

I rang his bell the next morning and had to ring several times before I saw him appear through the screen door, in his bathrobe again.

"I'll come back," I blurted.

"What is it?"

"I'm Erin Burke, Dr. Lyons. I've been coming on Saturdays and after school. If you need me—?"

He thought for a moment before he said, "Miss Efficiency. Yes." He smiled. "No, come in. Oh yes, I think you're greatly needed."

"I'll make coffee," I said, ingratiatingly. Miss Efficiency always made coffee. "I always did for Dr. Franklin, as long as his ration stamps lasted."

"In which case," he said, blushing, "I'll return dressed like a doctor."

I could hear his electric razor as I sat at the kitchen table while bubbles splashed in the little glass knob of the percolator on the range. I picked up the copy of the *Long Island Daily Press* that Dr. Lyons had brought in. On the page devoted daily to the news and photos of the area's servicemen, I read that the Cambria Movie House on Linden near the Canton Palace was being closed for the day—to honor the memory of the husband of Betty Leonard, the matron, as we called the usher in charge. The remains of John Leonard, who'd been missing in action, had been found in a trench full of prisoners that the Germans had machine-gunned in the Argonne Forest.

The remains of the dead were being shipped home to be reburied in Pinelawn Military Cemetery, out near the potato fields of Farmingdale.

On another page, there was an ugly photograph. A sewer pipe had backed up and caused a flood among the Quonset huts set up to house returning veterans in Canarsie. Ex-Mayor Fiorello La Guardia was furious, calling for an investigation of the contractors of the Defense Department. "It's bad enough," he told a press conference, "that they stick our heroes out there in the stink of Canarsie. This takes the cake."

There would be empty Quonset huts rusting years afterward, near the bulrushes of the swampy shores of Canarsie, where even the Lenape Indians, who sold Manhattan to the Dutch for sixty guilders' worth of trinkets, wouldn't have lived. It's not known how the government had the thought to put their recent heroes there, but they had to put a lot of them somewhere where there was land to install temporary housing. Thousands of married veterans were returning to where there had been almost no building since the Depression and none during the War. Slums everywhere had gone into unhealthy, unbearable decay. It's imaginable that someone far away, in Washington, rationalized that they were giving some lucky veterans a roof and also a view of the ocean, but the wind was not an ocean breeze…

So it was clear what getting out of Canarsie, at the bay where all the sewers of the city emptied, would mean to the limping friend eating with Jimmy at the Canton Palace with his wife and baby.

✺

A downpour of rain pinged on the metal roof with the insistence of an attack. For a second, Jimmy heard rifle fire, but the cry of the child behind a curtain took him to where he was now. In a moment, having hummed her daughter to sleep, Jacqueline Porter came out from behind the curtain and made coffee at the electric hotplate. Jimmy drank with something like hope that the caffeine would lift his spirits. Nobody spoke, but there was between them a gentle closeness so that time didn't need to be filled with saying, for them to define themselves further. Finally, the husband, Warren, spoke: "I've been everywhere and you know what they say to us wherever we look."

Jimmy shook his head.

"One thing: We're not going to stick our daughter up there with the rats in Harlem."

Jimmy reached his hand across the Formica table top.

Jacqueline gave him an inquisitive look. What could that gesture mean or promise from Warren's friend, a stranger to her until now? The "really nice White guy" Warren had met, both of them recuperating in France.

"You got a phone, Jacqueline?" Jimmy asked.

"There's one over at that office," she said. "Jimmy."

"Can you write down the number?"

Jimmy rose. It was late. He'd have to pick his way through the puddles in the dark outside.

After he'd said goodbye, the smell hit him again out there,

and the rain made it worse. It turned its immaterial self into a thicker presence that stayed on his jacket.

He cursed and headed where a bus, up the road, might still be coming.

On a damp wall back in there, Jacqueline, Warren's wife had pinned up a print of Van Gogh's Starry Night, which, with all its tormented rhythm, still might have assured her to believe that there was urgent beauty in the world.

Jimmy gave Sanford Rose the telephone number of the Quonset complex office the next morning...

ﻌﻬﻌ

Warren Porter remembered...

The Flak bursting in the sky of Saarbrücken like puffs of color. Fourth of July!

This is what really is, no holiday and the thing was to stay in the moment...An FW-190 pops up from below, crazy...I nod the B-51 down and the front cannon blasts him gone in a swirl of smoke and flame. The thought comes: They're not what they used to be. Not with the hotshot skill they had when I started out. Younger, no doubt, whomever they could get into the air and they go up with not a lot of fuel. Saarbrücken on fire down below. Then was twenty-eight times, there or wherever, from back in North Africa.

I'm going home with one more trip, to go really home, and they're gonna tell met it's thirty now. Thirty to hang up my helmet...

Bridge on the Saar... That's their home down there so they must be pretty mad—give them credit.

Our lead plane dips and turns. That's it. The B-17s have dropped their loads, and all aboard, we're going back...Not all of us: Four Fortresses on fire. Three no longer in the wide blue— Watch out: Another candidate. I give a machine gun burst and that pilot actually veers away. He doesn't like his job that fellow.

Turning home, turning home: the "fortresses," what was left of them, still stacked in staggered formation, like boxes one above the other and—the lead B-17 just bought it. I'm going home...but what they call a fortress, the one close isn't turning. The glamor girl's head and torso shot away, a cannon blow, and there are guys in there all over, other guys who'd been hit rushing to do something for them, and the pilot he can't see is still on course ahead, like he's off nowhere—something wrong with him all right.

I fly in front of him and wave my wings up and down. I could see his face now and I keep gesturing for him to turn home with the rest of everybody already well ahead...He turned, thank God, but now there are two bandits. I climb as hard as I could and maybe I'll pass out dizzy but I'm up there and behind one guy and shot him out of the sky and when the second guy turns, we're firing in each other's faces and that's it, I caught it! The Plexi blasted, a bullet in my leg and another in my groin that went through the flak suit, but my cannon won the match! And down the FW-190 goes. Down.

Bad pain, but suddenly, I'm calm. Like my plane and me, surviving together in loving devotion, no panic. I was in the moment and it was what was, all there was. And in my calm, all of a sudden, with all the other thoughts washed away, I hear poetry. And from stashed in my mind I hear it. Poetry. I hear, "I do not fight for those I love,"—their love *is not the issue here. And I hear, "The years behind a waste of time...When measured with this life, this death." So this was the glorious moment in the "heavens"—the mystical epiphany the instructor called it in the English class that in that one year at Tuskegee had me taking apart car motors and knowing poetry. Keep this death. I want more. A beautiful woman and a kid coming. And the rest to see. And then, it was now, the B-17 to shepherd and that was what there was to do. I stay shotgun near the crippled bomber, but the Nazi boys were gone, with enough fuel, they probably hoped, to get back to where I hoped an air field no longer existed. I led on, on course. Alone there in the B-51, not in anyone's sights now. Twenty-eight missions, three Messerschmidt-109s, and two FW-190s destroyed—including the new three. When this perilous, wounded way home has to have a happy ending...*

In time he saw the ground of the airfield. Slowly, slowly he went down behind the wounded fortress. It touched the field—and exploded! He nosed up quickly and there still was field enough for him to nose down again and land.

Captain Porter's medal came a week later in the hospital; a White Major came and brought it.

He called me son; he didn't call me boy. Maybe I was fighting for whom and what I may someday love. Like the country the Tuskegee professors professed to believe would someday be. But what is real now, don't mess with me, is that I am a man. Love me fellahs, or not.

༺࿐༻

He was Captain Warren Porter, brought up by illiterate share-cropping parents—as the PM daily newspaper would reveal—in an unpainted shack in Walker County Alabama, to where he had no intention of returning. He had been to many places since, before Cambria Heights. North Africa, Yugoslavia, Austria, Romania, Greece, Germany, all seen from way above.

Warren Porter had been a bright student in his one-room country school for Blacks and a similarly designated high school he'd walk to, shoeless for miles, rain or shine, and he had got a scholarship to Tuskegee Institute. Before his first year of automotive engineering was over, he knew he was going to war—and he wasn't going to go there to drive a truck. Tuskegee was chosen by the war department, softening their unrelenting Jim Crowism to train Blacks as war pilots. Porter jumped at the opportunity and became a talented learner. He was shipped to North Africa where he had the baptism of fighter combat piloting B-51s in the Mediterranean alongside flying fortresses bombing Italians. White or Black, the U.S. pilots had a good chance of dying before fulfilling their tour of duty, which began at twenty-five missions and was raised to thirty. But Porter ended his in a hospital near Paris, after he'd had five downed German fighter planes painted on the fuselage of his plane. He might have stayed there in Paris, if Jacqueline—who was from New York, whom he'd met at a USO dance before he'd shipped over—wasn't waiting for him to come back.

They had got married at Brooklyn Borough Hall before he left from New York to England. Had enough hotel time together for love, for her to be with child. He had a friend Darryl who opened a ribs restaurant in Paris after the War, marrying a White Frenchwoman. Paris was not Alabama, but Porter never gave a thought to not going back to his Jacqueline. Although, along with a lot of other returning G.I.s, he went home where there was no home to go to.

The government assigned them a Quonset hut to live in, at Canarsie. This time with no racial separation. They shared their awful discomfort equally.

FIVE

"**M**inna," Gus Loburg said, "Get a load of this!"

His wife lifted her head from cutting peonies to look to where her husband was watering their front lawn.

"A load of what?"

A bunch of kids had been playing stickball. They'd stopped and were looking down the street.

She saw, like they did, Jimmy King with a duffle bag on his shoulder. A thin, very young woman wearing glasses had a little baby—an infant—in her arms. The guy in the Ike jacket carrying a valise must have been the husband. *Blacks.*

Gus shook his head in disbelief.

Sanford Rose, the English teacher, a few lawns down, stopped mowing. He was wearing a pair of madras Bermudas, in a color that Gus believed no man would wear—he, who had the reputation of wearing what looked like the same tired gray double-breasted suit to all his classes. Gus frowned. He considered the teacher's garish outfit a provocation. *See, I'm different.*

Rose dropped the handle of his lawnmower and shook the hand of the Black man wearing the Ike jacket.

The kids stared a moment until the batter tossed a Spalding and hit it with his broomstick and they went on to their game.

I was coasting by on my bicycle on my way to Dr. Lyons when I saw Gus Loburg, standing with the hose while the spray was soaking his lawn. Across the street, the Black man in the Ike jacket and his wife holding her baby, were talking to Victoria and

Sanford Rose. Victoria kissed the woman on the cheek and took the infant in her arms, as they headed to the side door of the Rose's house, with the veteran Black soldier shouldering the duffel bag, alongside Jimmy.

Gus' lawn looked flooded.

꜀꜄

It was my grandmother Iris who dubbed Gustav Loburg our street's "nice Nazi"—a non-satirical, while precise perception that belonged to my grandmother's convictions about the ironies of living. Gus Loburg was what people today would call conflicted.

"If Hitler had only teamed up with the Jews," Gus had maintained more than once to the Siegals, on the other side of the white wooden fence between them, "nobody could have stopped them." The subtext of his explanation of that catastrophic mistake was his version of an apology—because he indeed liked the Siegals. There was no reason to believe that Gus was insincere in the friendship he pressed on his next-door neighbors, Blanche and Ivor Siegal. He rarely shared his opinions with anyone else on the street; it was, to him, as if the Jews and the Germans had a special, favorable relationship—a closeness—that concerned them and only secondarily concerned the rest of the world. Hitler had committed a dire misunderstanding of how that closeness should prevail; it had wrecked his place in history. He had his side of that story, and Hitler, whom Gus had reasons, all things said, to respect—he'd lifted Germany out of calamitous Depression—had his. It was a metaphysical story; ruling the world might have been divinely divided between the Germans and the Jews. Deaf in his left ear, almost deaf in the other, and so 4F, Gus never had to go to war and be in conflict with that. The Siegals, who had emigrated from Liverpool a few decades earlier, had North of England accents, which set them off from New York Jews. That was something more that Gus found admirable. He was an admirer, as well, of Winston Churchill. In the world of Gus Loburg's imagination, Jews, Germans and the British were getting along together, improving the world, all three of superior human stock. He had listened to the radio in March, when the former Prime Minister, in Missouri, rejected by his ungrateful people, spoke out against the Russians: "From Stettin in the Baltic to Trieste, an iron curtain has descended across the continent." Churchill wanted to give the Germans back their guns to defend the West against Bolshevism, already insinuating itself with what he'd called "fifth columns."

Loburg classed Hitler's animosity toward Jews as a misapprehension that devastatingly got out of hand, and he believed that it was, in the end, unconscionable. When Germany declared war on the United States after Pearl Harbor, he draped the doorway of his store in red, white, and blue crepe. My grandmother would sell him that day a hundred dollars in Victory Bonds.

The Siegals were a quiet old couple that wanted to get along with everybody, Good Germans as well as anyone. I think that they cherished some comfort in the fact that Jews, after all, had done so well among the Germans in the past. So I think they believed, in their version of denial, that deep down Gus was a Good German.

Gus' X sticker on the windscreen of his Chevrolet meant that his business exempted him from putting his car up on blocks for the Duration, as so many people on the street were obliged by law to do. In hot weather, Gus would invite the Siegals with their dog Trixie in tow to Lake Ronkonkoma to picnic with him and Minna. The Siegals, who were not religious, would enjoy Gus' gentile deli food, in particular Minna's potato salad. Gus would row them around while he fished for white perch.

Once, upon Minna's invitation to my grandmother, she and I went along on one of those boat rides. Minna had insisted that Iris bring nothing but "your lovely presence." On our street, my grandmother was an admired figure for her concerned while dignified gregariousness; at the same time Minna knew we were two creatures who spent our time alone together, and she reached out to offer us company with her hospitality. The Siegals came with freshly-baked strawberry shortcake. It was the season for strawberries. We had a picnic lunch on the shore. Gus had prepared sandwiches with Italian-style ham and the liverwurst he'd made himself. The adults drank beer and sweated while I had a very cold root beer from the chest in Loburg's trunk. The fish weren't biting, and with the languorous heat no one's mind seemed able to take them beyond small talk. We sat beside the lake; odd companions lazily congenial. It was like where we'd come, each from elsewhere in time and place: the hospitable couple with their idea of reformed Nazism, the gentle Jewish Siegals, my "proactive" as they now say patriotic grandmother, and innocent me. It was in the first week of June 1944 before Jimmy left. Were we living, with our congeniality, a tiny footnote about surprising complications in the story of human behavior on earth? It was cold that fateful week in Normandy.

Gus Loburg had a certain respect for the Lepke attachment of the Siegals. All things taken into account, Lepke was a man of exceptional influence in the world. When the OPA banned tinned dog food, Lepke was able to avoid upsetting Trixie with a strange, dry diet, having access to a black-market pre-war supply of Fido's Treat, which he would have delivered to the Siegals from an unmarked van that served whatever number of celebrities. Loburg never met Louis Buchalter to thank him for the X sticker for his car—a privilege beyond the one for his deli's delivery van—but he was thankful to the Siegals for that unlimited access to tires and gasoline. Lepke was a celebrity, and like other people in the neighborhood, Gus may have got some kind of rub-off of prestige from the proximity, faint as it was, to a celebrity. He had the same blind spot about Lepke's evil exceptionalness as he did regarding the Führer over there where his relatives lived and whence filial attachment to the Old Country still carried through to him.

I saw Lepke once. I was ten years old, and although our family knew through Grandma about his intermittent visits, I was prudently kept from knowing that. The man flinched as our back door opened across from his. I came out and saw the instant when he reached into a pocket of his velvet-collared coat. I saw a well-dressed man there with his dog, that I would come to know as Trixie. He turned to take her to the back yard, rather than the street, and as he hesitated and turned to look at me with my pail of garbage, he took off his hat and smiled, with the politeness that would honor an adult. I found his smile very sympathetic.

Gus Loburg's selective, self-redeeming vision of morality was no different from a lot of people's.

The Jewish Roses were another kettle of fish. Sanford Rose would even take time from his English lessons at Jackson to bestow leftist talk on his students. He had them learning about the American Revolution through the eyes of Howard Fast, the communist novelist. He wore weird shorts at home in colors suitable for a woman, when he wasn't at school in those famous shabby suits. Gus had heard about Rose at Jackson from some unhappy customers who were parents. Gustav Loburg's not having joined the American Nazis' Bund was testimony of his patriotism in the country that had allowed him and Minna a good living—proof that it even exceeded his measured admiration for Adolph Hitler— while Sanford and Victoria Rose's door to door canvassing for the American Labor Party made them obvious fellow-travelers of the dangerous Fifth Column of Joseph Stalin. Gus steered clear of having anything to do with his close neighbor, the subversive egghead Sanford Rose.

Sanford and Victoria Rose would pitifully be cannon fodder in what came to be called the Cold War, but, while Alex Franklin opened his library to me, the Sanford Rose I knew, with chalk on the sleeves of his tired double-breasted jacket when he read to us out loud, making notes on his blackboard, was a conjurer of observations who made words on paper release a compelling presence of life.

From that passion he showed when he read us poetry, we could know that one generation away from his parents' world of pogroms, humiliation, and terror, Sanford Rose's heart had bonded with love to an exhilarating situation. He was the best teacher I have ever had, and so many of us in his class felt that way. At the same time his intellect, as if having learned reasons for many things in his studies, concluded that the ontology of human life had a design intending it for a utopia. Sanford Rose was at once an accolade of the Western world's high culture and a Marxist enemy of its social structure—like his parents who came to America as refugees from a terrorized shtetl, and knew it was a refuge. All the while, his parents, who weaned his intellect on Marxism, had dreamed of its destruction and rebirth—a secular heaven—beyond all its irrefutable injustices.

Sanford Rose had his Stalin leading the way. Loburg, though he was no intellect embracing Hitler's philosophy, had, he thought, a common-sense admiration for the Führer.

And Lepke, CEO of Murder Incorporated, no philosopher, with his brain wildly wired with a fanatical conviction about how the world was, in which nice guys definitely finished last, loved his wife, his in-laws, and his dog Trixie.

Maybe each, so different and in some ways alike, was finally who he was through the luck of the draw. And not any of them, nor James King D.D., nor Father Gerry Maloney could reveal how the

Dealer shuffled his cards. The best those two could do was to confirm that the creator of the intricate universe found no amusement in doing anything simply.

We, his students, had much to admire in Sanford Rose's mind and heart. Rather than a public enemy, a Fifth Columnist of Gus Loburg and Winston Churchill's description, he was, as I remember him, an endearing human of moral impulse, who only a few years later would know a traumatic loss of innocence and change his life when Nikita Khrushchev blew the whistle about Stalin. But in the frightened, inquisitional time just ahead, not any of us nor anyone could save Sanford Rose the subversive egghead from disgrace. All this was the America I knew…

As for Black people, Gus Loburg believed that it was an empirically proven fact that they were of a less-advanced order of humanity than Whites. He had, he'd say, no predisposition to hate rather than disdain them. The latter was just an obvious conclusion: What had they contributed to the civilization of the Western world other than what some people called music? Three young Blacks had held him up at gunpoint in his delicatessen one morning, and taken three hundred dollars from his register. One of them was crazily excited and threatened to kill him. That event was—in a paradoxical sense—a gift to his understanding. It had enriched his disdain with unexpired anger. But Gus also clung loyally to what was the law, as much so as an SS camp guard had unquestionably been loyal to his Führer. That moral virtue of discipline was in counterpoint with his bitter dismay, that day, on my second weekend morning working for Dr. Lyons, when Gustav stood watering his lawn and looking at that Black man in the army jacket on which Loburg could still make out a patch with a leopard spitting fire on it.

ళ్ళ

Soon after, the pastor and the delicatessen man had a brief conversation while watching King's Little League practice. Gustav Loburg's twins were playing; Tim hit a ball deep into left field, where his brother Mike made a great catch.

"Your kids are talented," King said. "How old are they?"

"Twelve. Not bad for twelve?"

"Not bad at all…"

Loburg changed the small talk:

"Reverend, I'm a Lutheran, and we go over to Queens Village to pray."

Pastor King wasn't expecting that declaration. It seemed an overture to saying something else.

"I know your Reverend Mehl," King said.

"He's from the same city as my family."

"Where is that, Gustav?

"Karlsruhe. Have you ever been to Germany?"

"I got as far as France."

"In the war? The first one?"

"In the war to end all wars."

"Well I'm glad at least that this one had ended. You have a son. Your son is a hero. How is he now?"

"He was convalescent when he came home," King answered.

"He's... okay..."

"You see the thing in my ear? I was 4F," Loburg said.

King glanced at the hearing aid.

There was a moment of silence before Loburg said: "I never joined the Bund, Pastor. I was taken once to the big rally in Madison Square Garden and I heard Hitler's Fritz Kuhn speak. That's all. There is one thing though," Loburg said, "I can't forget. I want to know what you, think, Pastor."

"Of what?"

"It happened in the spring of '42."

"What happened?"

"Someone rang my bell."

"Rang your bell?"

"In the middle of the night. It was my cousin, Dieter. My uncle's son."

"In the middle of the night? What did you do?"

"I gave him our couch to sleep on until the next morning."

"A cousin is a cousin," King said. He was getting uncomfortable about hearing another family crisis. He'd heard plenty in his parish.

"Do you want to know how he got there?"

"Did that matter?"

"Yes. He got off a submarine in Sheepshead Bay, got into a

rubber boat, got off near a subway, spent a nickel, and when he got to the last stop on our way, he stole a bike and rang my bell."

King stared at him. "You mean?"

"He got off a submarine."

"What did he say?"

"He asked about what was going on over here. Maybe he did what he did just because he was instructed to see if he could."

"And he didn't do anything else?"

"Nothing. Nothing. He had breakfast and left. If he did something bad, you would have read about it."

"What did you tell him?"

"That everything here was going excellently. That no one could ever take over this country."

"He believed you?"

"He was impressed. Should I have told the FBI? And what would they make of me? Did I do something bad?"

"A cousin is a cousin," King said, not open to anything more priestly with Loburg. "Have you heard from him since?"

"I heard from the family after the war. His boat got hit by depth charges a year later, in the North Sea…Was I not a patriot not to have told the FBI? I'm an American citizen," Loburg said. "My wife has her citizenship. But you know, you can never turn your back on *your race*."

"I hope your son is feeling better," Loburg said to King's back, already turned as he headed toward his Packard.

❧

The kids in the street told their parents and the Black family's arrival became an event known to all. When the ladies in my Grandma's gin rummy club came to our house that week, their klatch took on elements of a crisis conference.

"It's serious," Teresa Fortunato said. "I don't have a problem with their presence, personally, believe me. Everybody is a human bean. But you know what's gonna happen."

"Don't tell me. The real estate people," Wanda Nowak replied, "are all over us. He gets one person that won't stay and one by one, everybody sells. You have to or you wind up the only Whites."

"There goes the neighborhood, bingo all colored," Bernadette Williams concurred. "And what happens to the value of your home you struggled so hard for? It becomes bupkis."

"What?" said Teresa.

"You know. It's a Jewish word," said Wanda.

"Where does Jewish come into this?" protested Teresa, "I have great esteem for the Siegals. Even the Loburgs love them."

"Bupkis" Bernadette insisted. "It's goat doo-doo resembling beans. My husband's lousy Jewish boss uses the word all the time."

My grandmother Iris sat there shuffling the cards almost violently. She poured every one of the ladies the much-anticipated glass of orange soda.

"You said…" she finally spoke. "You said it. Everybody's a human *being*. And everybody's got to act like one. Why do you think—whatever his name is—the colored GI was limping?

What do you think he got shot up for, doing that in a bigger way than any of us could ever do? I like it here. I'll stay. I'd be comfortable, so to speak, dying on 240th Street."

There was silence. Iris dealt the cards. Iris loved to deal…

⁓

Warren Porter had his head under the hood of Dr. Lyons' Hudson, revving the carburetor in what looked like a tune-up, when I drove into the driveway on my bicycle to begin my afternoon. A Checker Cab was parked in front of Dr. Lyons' house with the motor turned off, and the driver was reading a newspaper. It was hot, and Porter was sweating in a khaki t-shirt. Before I could say hello, a woman's shouting came out of the house.

Porter said, "I wouldn't go in there."

We heard:

"I'm finally going to have a life!"

We didn't hear Lyons' answer.

"He understands me. I love him!"

I just stood there, and Porter stopped revving the engine.

"I want to have children!"

"I wanted to have children," Dr. Lyons said in a flat voice. He wasn't arguing; it was as if an argument was of no use in proving anything. He was repeating a stale story.

"I wouldn't have children with a drunkard!"

"I've gone off it, Dorothy."

"There's enough here to drive anyone to drink, Cato! What kind of life? A doctor who does house calls in a neighborhood of losers. And I get what? I want a divorce, once and for all."

"And the horses?" were her last words in mockery, before a long silence. From the driveway, I heard the front screen door slam. I looked back and saw a well-dressed blonde wearing a straw hat get into the taxi. The driver put down his newspaper with a look of relief, started his engine and drove off.

"I'm almost finished," Porter said. "Doc can pay me another time. I am not going in there."

I stood there a moment, looking at the taxi driving away. So few people came in taxis to our street, that the taxi itself seemed to me an intrusion, with the same resentment that came over me about the blonde.

I hesitated, but I went in. It was my duty to be there then, I hadn't given a reason for not coming. And it was as if my going forth into the routine might make things normal again.

Dr. Lyons wasn't in his office. From the center hall, I could see into the dining room. He didn't see me. He was sitting at the dining room table, where Mary had put food on two plates—both untouched—and I remembered that she'd mentioned that he'd asked her to get his blazer out of his closet and give it a press. I think it was the best thing in his wardrobe.

He didn't see me. I don't know what he saw in his mind's eye, as he sat there and stared ahead at another place, a moment of another Apollonian civilization, in a print of a Renoir's café scene on a wall across the table. Beside him was an ashtray already full of butts.

"The horses?" echoed strangely in my mind.

⚜

I hadn't been to Coney Island since I was a kid when my father had driven us while I sat in the rumble seat of his Reo coupe that would later sit on blocks for the Duration. I had agreed, unrealistically to go to Coney with Jimmy, in a sort of denial, as if it belonged to the easy way we've been before. As if maybe we could even get back to that. We took the subway this time. Pastor King wasn't lending his son the Packard again, and I don't know whether my being the designated passenger had something to do with that.

We went for the amusement park instead of the beach. Who needed the beach at Coney—covered with people—when you had Jones Beach?

The subway entrance was back among the rickety boarding houses. We got out with a horde—shouting kids, people carrying umbrellas and beach chairs. When we passed the beach, there seemed to be no more room for all of them. It was blanket to blanket, no matter that the public had been warned that crowded beaches might well be a place to catch polio.

As we walked along the boardwalk, the smell of burnt wood began to inhabit the sea air. We came to Luna Park. A whole section of it was all burnt out. The scenery of the Scenic Railway looked as if a bomb had fallen and left a charred crater. Jimmy stood there a minute and his shrug became a shudder, and then he tugged my arm and led me away until we came to Steeplechase Park. Steeplechase had burnt too, years ago, but it had been built again and was now full of excited people. People were bouncing as they raced, clinging to mechanical horses while the tracks led to a stretch as high as the middle of the Ferris wheel. "Half a mile in half a minute and fun all the way!" a barker was shouting over the screams of people up there and over on the roller coaster. Kids looked up in every direction, astounded faces smeared with cotton candy. We'd walked into a happy world that had tamed danger into fun. Jimmy seemed very brightened, very up. He said, "Let's take the roller coaster." The minute he mentioned it I felt a pang of nausea. "I'll watch you," I said. He looked at me just a second and headed for the ticket office, looking back, beaming.

You don't get a long ride. He was back. He wanted to know what would "excite" me. I was just happy to watch all of it. I said, "Okay, let's take some kooky ride." When we swept through the Tunnel of Love, I got a mandatory long kiss. The boat deposited us at the Earthquake Stairway and he tugged me onto the Human Roulette Wheel, where again I was nauseated. But at the same time I was happy. I was happy, yes, that he was happy. We'd left not only Cambria behind that day, but also everything else. Our lives—what had changed them. It was all fun and thrills, and the danger wasn't real; it was indeed a metaphor of danger turned into a version of pleasure. We were hungry, and we stopped at Nathan's and ate frankfurters with mustard and sauerkraut, as mouthwatering as they were before the war. And French fries that were greasy and sweet and somehow tasted good as well.

On the subway ride home, we had to stand and hang onto the straps. It was crowded, hot, and smelly. I wondered whether we were risking catching polio. He asked finally, "Are you sorry?"

I didn't answer—I didn't give an answer because I hadn't one. I had changed. He was responsible. So was I. Should I tell him I was in no way happy about it? Would it have mattered if I asked him, "Are you sorry?" Maybe I should have, maybe I didn't because I didn't know whether it was an unpitying provocation to find out whether that emotion fit him in his life now. We didn't talk after his unanswered question, not even to break the silence, banally, about the time that the Q4 bus took to leave from the 168th Street IND station.

He kissed me goodbye at the door of my house, in a way that made it seem that we were just good friends again. He seemed, anyway, somewhere else, and he didn't look like it was now a happy place.

But then, as I turned to go in, he spun me around and ran his hands all over me, with a frenzy. I clamped my mouth against his tongue. I broke away, truly afraid of what he intended to do again, there on my doorstep.

He turned and left me.

From the light of the lamppost in front of Sanford Rose's place, I had seen splashes of black all along the walk and on the screen door.

Jimmy was standing now in front of the Rose's darkened house. He drew his finger across a splattered screen door.

Our whole street would have something big to think about.

For me, it would all be a time of reprieve, if I could give it that meaning, from stubbornly returning thoughts about where things ultimately, insuppressibly, were to be between Jimmy and me.

჻

It was evening and the Embers Lounge was lowly lit to create the atmosphere of a lair, a shelter from whatever was too sharp—too strident—in life outside. The alcoholic's womb world, the unbinding ambience of the social drinker. More light from streetlamps flowed in as Jimmy came through the door. He closed it in a hurry, as if out there was pursuing him.

He saw Cato Lyons. Dr. Lyons was standing at the bar with a shot and a beer and the way he stared bleakly into the mirror behind the bar, you could surmise that it wasn't his first drink in front of him. Jimmy sat down on the stool beside him. They were the only two people there with Louie, the corpulent bartender, who might have also been a bouncer at one time, but he'd gone from impressively built to obese.

Jimmy didn't speak at first, and Louie thought it appropriate to break the heavy silence by turning on the radio behind him. Not with music, because the coin-eating juke box in a corner of the room had the designated monopoly on that. He switched through a whirl of noise until he settled his dial where an evening's episode had just come on with its introduction:

"Who knows what evil lurks in the hearts of man?" Louie repeated.

"Say it once again," Jimmy finally said.

Louie looked like he'd made a mistake.

Lyons drank down his shot and sipped his beer.

"The Shadow knows," the radio voice went on…

"I used to listen to that all the time as a kid," Jimmy said. "It scared the heck out of me."

He'd addressed Lyons with the air of creating friendly conversation, but Louie sensed he was in a state that made him think the young guy had come here after drinking elsewhere. He offered a banality to create some bonhomie.

"I listen all the time to a lot of that thriller stuff," said Louie.

"Doesn't scare you?" Jimmy said, with an overtone of sarcasm.

Louie felt the tone, and answered back, "What scares you?"

"Heavy ordnance," Jimmy said. "The whistle of big rounds."

Louie changed his attitude. "You've been there," he said, with respect. "I was too old."

Lyons turned toward the young man. His voice had a diffident tone, too.

"Where?" he asked.

"The other side of the moon," Jimmy said.

"Which theater?"

"That's some term to describe it…Europe, the whole works." He allowed himself a beat to hear Lyons say more. "You know?" he asked.

"The Pacific. I wasn't too old for what they had me do."

Jimmy noticed Lyons' hand had a faint twitch as he lifted his shot glass. "The Marines?" he asked gently.

Jimmy waited discreetly for Lyons to define the rest.

"I'm a navy doctor with them. Was."

"I guess you saw stuff."

"I presume you killed people and I patched people up and we were each in our way, doing his part in what had to be done," Lyons pronounced.

"You saw stuff?" he asked gently, but it was more like a word of commiseration than a question.

The defensiveness that hung over Jimmy was suddenly gone. He put his arm on Louie's sleeve. "What did I ask for?" he said, and he made it sound like it was a question that resonated in his life beyond the Embers Lounge.

"You forgot. You forgot to order," Louie said complacently.

"I'll follow the good doctor," Jimmy said, "a boilermaker."

Louie had a thought again that the kid had come in already a few sheets to the wind, but he didn't make waves—wouldn't just yet—and served a Four Roses and a Rheingold.

Jimmy drank down the shot and turned to Lyons.

"I see it all the time now. I can't stop seeing it."

"You've got to put it behind."

"You believe that? You're doing that? Where were you?"

"Tarawa, for one."

"Jesus Christ, Doctor, what can you do with your life after—" He didn't finish his sentence.

"Where were you?" Lyons insisted, "Call me Cato."

"A great republican. He hated Caesar."

"He killed himself…" Cato drank down the rest of his beer.

"All over Europe. And I was at Dachau, when we liberated it. I don't know what I'm going to do. It's all grey territory ahead of me."

"You're the pastor's son? Jimmy? Erin Burke mentioned you."

"What did she say?"

"You've been out together."

"Excuse me, you have a woman, Cato?"

"Had."

"Had. That's how it goes."

"What do you mean?"

"People. Tell me about people loving each other. Look what they've been doing on the scale they've been doing it. Excuse me, I didn't mean anything if she...died."

"Left. She wants a divorce. I'm drinking off the experience."

"That was what I'm saying. You get involved with somebody and sorrow occurs."

"You guys quenched your thirst?" Louie was worried. Things had become somber; the two of them looked like they were heading for a funeral or had just been to one. This kind of scene in a bar sometimes winds up in a fight.

"You know about it, Jimmy?"

Jimmy sensed a patronizing tone in the doctor's voice, or maybe it was just the alcohol that made him say any old thing.

"Truth to tell. My hand on the Bible? I find it all confusing, human nature. I had a buddy who didn't come back. He liked to dilute his fear with sayings: 'Where there's people, there's danger.'"

Louie switched his radio station. "It's Henry Aldrich time," he announced as if he were bestowing them something that would make things appreciative and convivial.

"Henry! Henry Aldrich!" Lyons said.

"Coming mother!" Jimmy chimed back. He heard the voice of the emblematic good son, the innocent, carefree star in a radio fantasy. In a world of trivia.

"Pathetic," Jimmy said.

"It's Henry Aldrich time in America, Louie," Jimmy said.

It sounded like a very bitter renunciation. Dr. Lyons could perceive free-floating anger persistently coming off Jimmy like a smell.

He looked Jimmy up and down, as if examining him. A little as if Jimmy were a patient, "Your Pop knows about love," he said. "He's a great generalist on the subject, no offense." He waited to hear revealed what might be the cause of a symptom.

Jimmy went elsewhere. "You see the tar?" he asked.

"The tar?"

"On the Roses' house."

"About the Blacks moved in. A war hero man and wife and baby. It's the same old world we fought against, am I right Doctor?" He held out his finger still stained.

"Believe me, doctor, whoever did it would be happy to be wearing a black uniform. All over Roses' door and sidewalk because my friend is living there now. Warren Porter? You know him."

"Fixed my car. What the—" Lyons exclaimed.

"Something wrong?" Louie asked.

༈

We never found out who splashed the tar at night. It was Grandma who remembered that the Loburgs, who left that morning to go upstate, always set forth for the long trip before dawn, to beat the truck-plagued traffic.

But there was no evidence pointing to anyone.

So, our ordinary street acquired importance beyond its boundaries, for a second time, after Lepke's secret visits. A man from the *Long Island Press*, a reporter, and a guy with a Speed Graphic from the *New York Daily Mirror* all three showed up shortly after two policemen in a squad car. People came out of their houses when they saw the police car and a crowd gathered around the Roses' place. The Siegals looked very distressed. They were probably reminded of newsreels in the thirties showing how the Nazis began persecuting Jews by smearing their property in black. But it was obvious that it wasn't because Sanford Rose was a Jew that the tar was suddenly all over the front of his house.

Jimmy looked furious. That look seemed intuitively to bother my grandmother; she seemed somehow apprehensive, as she looked at me.

"Where's the colored guy?" one of the policemen asked Rose.

Just then, Warren Porter stepped out and looked at the crowd like a camera panning the scene. People whispered and nudged each other.

"He have enemies?" the cop persisted.

"Of course," Rose said, "Warren Porter was born with enemies."

The policeman noticed Porter now, but kept on talking to Rose, as if to prepare that guy's questioning.

"So you can tell me about this person? You checked him out before you rented to him?"

"Are you interested in who might be the person who threw the tar?" Rose asked. His tone was getting more irritated.

"We're interested in knowing as much as we can that can matter."

Porter, who'd been silent, walked up slowly to the cop. People stared at his limp. He was close to the cop's face.

"What's there to know?" He half-turned and looked at us. "It's all there in black and white." He walked back inside and slammed the door.

An old Plymouth coupé pulled up and a young guy with rimless glasses stepped out. The reporters from the *Mirror* and the *Press* seemed to return grudgingly the nod he gave them. He showed the police his press card for the afternoon daily called P.M. P for "pinko" people liked to say. He looked around for someone to comment and went up to Rose. Rose had his words prepared.

"We fought a war against fascism, but as you can see, the war is not over. The racism that Adolph Hitler preached—am I going too fast?—has yet to be defeated in our own country. I don't know who perpetrated this offense, but he is only a tool, you know, of the forces that deliberately foment racism, so as to keep the working people divided—angry at each other, when they should deal with those who exploit them."

"I'd like to speak to your new tenant," the reporter said.

"Warren Porter. P-o-r-t-e-r. He has authorized me to speak for him."

"What did he tell you to say?"

"I just said it."

"Do you have enemies?"

"It's plain who that tar is aimed at. Warren and Jacqueline just moved in."

All of us, not just a culprit, were now attached to the event. People bit their lips. We were simple people with simple lives, battered for years by shockwaves of distant violence, and here was a hostile event, freighted with meaning, right on our sidewalk glaring at us, no matter what any of us thought of Blacks.

Next day page one of the P.M. read: "Racial Unrest in Queens."

The police who were taken by Gustav Loburg's German name thought he might have had a motive for the deed. They wanted to question him, but he and Minna had been away on a week's vacation to Lake George, upstate. There was a hotel there renowned for its Sauerbraten, with a Bavarian band and a dance floor. Gus and Minna danced there when he managed time off. Gus in the Italian-made light shoes that Ivor Siegal had passed on to him, which had been passed onto Ivor. Lepke's dancing shoes, that he'd had made on a pre-war trip to colleagues in Italy. Gus felt something like a confirmation of his belief in his pro-Semitism in that his feet fit the shoes of the brother of a rabbi…who was electrocuted for murder.

Billy Nowak, whose Montauk run for the *Daily News* brought him home early in the morning, was the only one who might have seen what happened…or done it. Questioned, he gave no evidence of either. Nor did he seem to have a strong motive.

The police did not come back.

SIX

Looking back now, I wish that someone could have been close to Cato Lyons, to help him in what he was going through. I was just his girl on Fridays, doing the motions of a secretary and coffee-maker, too young to interfere in a life that I could not help but perceive to be in trouble. "On the skids" is that term they use for alcoholics, but he was there sometimes— brilliantly steady, carefully devoted with his patients; other times, when alone, he was not there—emotionally racked in a conflict that he fought to survive.

Sometimes when I came into his living room, where for me Dr. Franklin was still a ghostly presence, I could smell alcohol. But his patients never knew him to be other than on top of things. After the alcohol, he'd smoke a lot and the effluvium of evidence was gone. That was far from the worst of my perceptions of his distress. After that visit from his estranged wife, I could not help but overhear the phone calls.

Who can really understand what unites two people inti-mately—what's the little centripetal implosion that occurs or the slow growth of a closeness whose coming apart will wound deeply? To say that every case is different is a cliché observation, but I have never read about a constant in all that. I read once that there was some presence beneath the level of perception of a smell that a woman or a man gives off to a potential mate that will be the elixir that starts a bond. But that doesn't go far beyond sexual attraction. I'm wondering about things more perilously complex, more consequential, all said, and also more fragile.

So you hear, "What did she see in him?" or "What did he see in her?" I never knew what Cato Lyons saw in his wife, and I had very little to go on to know about her. I believe that their coming together was a great, destructive act of fate in his life. I think that the war, with all its calamity was all the same no more than another catalyst to that.

It was one of I don't know how many marriages that the war created or was their fateful intrusion. I think that people met and the dire times gave a kind of energy to their coming together—discovering that the other was something defiantly, excitingly good in that moment, when an overwhelming threat of the worst was definitely personal. You married defiantly: No matter what, we loved, we united, in that union that had the gravitas of a consecration. All the more meaningful because so fragile, endangered. Let's make it be—let's be sure of obtaining ownership of that exalted thing, because we aren't sure that one of us won't be back. So it was fragile, too, because all that emotion may have been different from love, from understanding. You could unfeelingly call it fool's gold. It was what they felt. Intensely. I am guessing about Cato Lyons' ill-fated case.

I heard him once later on the telephone: "Dorothy, couldn't we reel everything back?" There was no loud answer coming out of his phone. In the silence I could hear the clink of ice in a glass.

Then she hit him again. I could hear right through the phone. "I love him!"

"While I was where I was…" He didn't finish the thought that came out.

I thought: 4F. The mouse will play. I was deeply on his side. But to be honest with himself, which doesn't always help, he'd no doubt have to do an excruciating inventory of his own incapacities and misunderstandings, for the sum of the story. But who am I to judge? I didn't know that sum.

Once again, I hear myself screaming the day that rendered all this irrelevant.

꙳

At Jamaica Hospital, where Cato Lyons spent one day a week, two White children had come in with what looked like the beginning of infantile paralysis. A boy of eight from Floral Park and a seven-year-old girl from Jamaica Estates. Nice, clean, well-off Queens neighborhoods. Fever, muscle pain, chills. By the time Lyons ended his shift at the end of the day, the affliction was a certainty in both cases.

Mary had left him a dish of cold fried chicken and potato salad. He drank water with it, but after he finished his canned fruit cocktail, he went to a kitchen cabinet, took out a bottle of scotch and looked at it sitting on the table. More? He knew that if he opened it, it would be like swimming out so far that there was no going back, and he also knew what he had to expect—no shore. The choice was still there, like to raise his arm or not. He raised it and reached for the bottle and poured himself a generous drink in his water glass. Dorothy would have confirmation regarding her take on things by the time he'd had a few more. Which he did.

The scotch eased him of his own grief and his mind traveled back to the hospital. And just then, as if it were a sign of some plan operating on his particular life that wasn't what he willed, the phone rang.

"Dorothy?" he said—the scotch said. But he knew better.

It was a nurse at the hospital, "Dr. Barossa has taken ill, doctor."

"What's wrong with him?"

"He just called in sick. There's no one to take his place."

"Now?"

"I'm afraid so."

"Okay."

"You're sure?"

He wasn't sure that it would be easy now for him to drive to Jamaica, but he said, "I'm sure." He'd been in far worse situations. The scotch knew.

The streets were clear of coming-home traffic. He drove the Hudson gingerly, but deftly. It actually seemed to him that the several drinks had loosened him in a way that his movements were smoother, more coordinated, as he shifted and down-shifted, stopped and started at lights, until he turned the car into the lot of the hospital.

The two polio victims were in an isolation ward.

"What's been done to them?" he asked the nurse. She was a plump, dark woman of about forty. She must have kids, herself, he thought. The Italians had lots of kids. Dorothy had none. Might just still with what's his name.

She shrugged and gave him a knowing look of frustration.

"Hot packs," she said.

What was there to do?

I was filing when Dr. Lyons came home from that visit. He looked devastated, and I could not ignore the smell of alcohol that wasn't medicinal. I brought him a coffee without asking, and he sat down, and took my hand to stay. He spoke:

"I went into the isolation ward. This little girl…she had her blanket in her mouth, chewing down on pain. Nighttime for healthy little girls is supposed to be filled with dreaming of sugar plums or whatever.

"I uncovered the blanket, rolled up her pajama leg. It was red—where the hot pack had been applied—no doubt a long time. The smell of wet wool was still in the air. Steamed army blankets, covered with cotton blankets, my God in the twentieth century. What was there to do? I checked the boy, who was just staring at the ceiling, as if he were in shock. More red flesh. What was there to do?

"The little girl began to cry. Someone had left a book on her bedside table. It was a book of fairy tales. So I read to her:

"Once upon a time, there lived a little girl whose father had married a widow with two daughters. Her stepmother didn't like her one bit…"

Why had he begun to tell a sad story to the poor kid? The world was flooded with sad stories and even kids learned that fast. Cato will get her to its happy ending. And her own?

He said, "I looked back at the boy. I saw him smile."

Cato Lyons was reminded that bravery was another verifiable truth in the world he had known. And that he needed to get in touch with it again, personally. Or drown. He resolved to keep swimming...

꙳

The news came on page one of the *Long Island Press*. Another small story, inside; this kind of news was long commonplace. But for us, it was a fearful portent. Laurelton was just across an avenue from Cambria Heights and the plague never needed any great distance to spread.

A boy of ten had been taken from Laurelton to Mary Immaculate Hospital in Jamaica, where he was diagnosed with infantile paralysis. His name was Stephen Grossman, an honor student at P.S. 156, the son of Myron Grossman, who had a large pharmacy on Merrick Road, in Laurelton just at the edge of Cambria. That a pharmacist had nothing in his vast inventory of cures to help his son made the story seem all the more poignant. But nobody in all of America, neither pharmacist nor doctor nor revered scientist had the cure. The boy was already in an iron lung.

"They ask you over and over to give to the March of Dimes," his father was quoted saying, "What are they doing with the money? My son can't move."

Myron Grossman's pharmacy, where the donation folder with dime-size holes on his counter that had been filled many times, was closed. He and his wife, Ruth, were put in quarantine. But no one in America knew whether that meant anything. People in Laurelton who used to buy their medicine at Grossman's were obliged to go to Wilkes' Drug Store in Cambria. In Cambria, a lot of residents became fearful that the plague might be spread that way.

No one knew how indeed polio was spread. Someone, I don't know who or where, came up with that idea that wearing those little sachets of camphor around your neck could ward off infection, and so a lot of mothers sewed those little sacks, and Wilkes' had a run-on camphor. Some mothers gave their kids little cloth gloves in case they touched the wrong thing. Since the disease was believed in any case to be contagious, somehow spread from person to person, the medical profession offered what it could, an admonition: stay away from crowds.

In the week that followed the news about Stephen Grossman, seven more cases of polio were reported in Laurelton. After the weekend, the Senior Prom Committee of Andrew Jackson High held an emergency meeting with our principal, Dr. Mildred Smallwood. There would be no hot crowd on the dance floor of the Empire Hotel in the City for the graduating class of Andrew Jackson of 1946. Mrs. Smallwood cancelled the reservation of the ballroom.

Jimmy cancelled the tux.

SEVEN

All this time something was happening in me that would fatally impinge on my life, but I was going on, thinking and pushing back my thoughts—as if everything could be patched like a cured wound and a piece of time could just be forgotten. Until, as if something more and more malignant, the question became insuppressibly there. Because, ready or not, it came with no shred of happiness meant naturally to be, and it had to have meaning and consequence.

We were two women at breakfast. One was me, a woman—a new person now. I didn't tell her. I couldn't tell anyone. But I was changed, and the change wasn't an exhilarating event, I had entered a place where I hadn't been, hadn't known, and it didn't seem to me that I had in any way enriched my existence. I'd been only fifteen when Jimmy left for the war. Now something had happened like the rising of sap in spring, but love? My empathy, admiration, and pity for the Jimmy who'd come home were irrepressible, but the thing that defined the difference was that I didn't feel a need—not wholly like a gift but also a burden—and it would hurt if the need weren't answered. I still can't define all that defines love, but I didn't feel the two-edged presence of possession and devotion of what it seemed to me love was—which I would never know until Walter became my husband years later.

If love had blossomed in me there under the stars at the beach, with my taste of passion, I would have felt that I'd been gifted; instead I was like someone who'd climbed a peak and didn't have the footing to go back.

My grandmother might have been the best person to talk to about it. I just couldn't get the courage. Grandma Iris was a spirited woman. She'd grown up in Hell's Kitchen, working class Irish, daughter of a patrolman. Her father had given her an attachment to righteousness beyond Catholic piety. She'd carried a placard marching with the women who finally got the right to vote in 1920. She'd voted for James M. Cox, against Warren Harding, drawn to Cox's running mate, Franklin D. Roosevelt, and when the time came, she would vote for FDR as president and again two more times. My grandmother tore out the flowers in our back yard for a Victory Garden, where she grew tomatoes and beans. She became a Minute Maid, ringing doorbells up and down Cambria to get people to buy war bonds, or even just those stamps that could accumulate into bonds. The butcher at his stall in Bohack's would hide the meat when he saw her enter the supermarket. There were other customers who paid him black market prices, but my grandmother would not offer a cent more than the war efforts of the Office of Price Administration made legal. We ate a lot of chicken, and Grandma Iris would dutifully go back to the butcher with the fat that remained, from our sparse meals of beef. The butcher would give her back the required four cents a pound for her jarful of proto-nitroglycerine with a smirk. When she wasn't doing her part for victory over evil, Grandma took pleasure in selling candy, part time, to children at the candy counter in Woolworth's on Jamaica Avenue.

My grandmother had indeed clear ideas of right and wrong. She took pleasure in listening to "Gangbusters" on the radio, where they recounted true examples of criminals earning punishment during the fifteen-minute episodes that began with the sound of marching prisoners, steel doors slamming—all of it that used to scare the life out of me.

She was warm-hearted, with all the affection I could expect from a mother while she cared for me—just the two of us together, while my mother was far away.

If there were anyone I should have told about what happened, it should have been her. I thought about how my grandmother was a good friend of—a good friend *to* the Siegals. Who needed one, she'd told me once, after our listening to Gangbusters. It had been the day the Siegals came home from Sing-Sing, where they'd driven (in Betty's red Cadillac convertible we'd seen on her visits to her parents) to be there for their daughter, on her mission to say goodbye to Louis. The night they executed him. Blanche wept in our kitchen the next day. I was fifteen, and for me, overhearing her story, with the excuse of coming in for a chocolate milk, brought on a little of the quiver of listening to Gangbusters. Everyone had read about Lepke's wild cruelty in his professional life. But Blanche looked back in her mind with blinders, recounting about the night she and Ivor, dressed in the evening clothes that were part of their son-in-law's largesse, were taken in a limousine to the Riobamba nightclub she owned, for a memorable supper and show. Betty's young discovery, named Frank Sinatra, dressed with the bowtie that had been her inspiration came out, trembling with stage fright until he crooned "Night and Day" and "She's Funny that Way" and brought down the house.

If Grandma could listen without any reproach to Lepke's mother-in-law weeping over his fate, despite the blood he'd spilled—blood still being thicker than water—if there were anyone with vast compassion to tell about what happened to me, it should have been my grandmother. I couldn't get it out.

We sat in the breakfast nook of our kitchen that next morning. Eating toast with apple butter—butter was still scarce on the shelves of Bohack's—and soft-boiled eggs, drinking the dark tea that was a part of her Irishness, and talking about the weather.

"You look troubled," she did say.

I just drank my tea. I couldn't make up a lie to answer her but I couldn't tell the truth either. I was troubled. I had a feeling that I had betrayed my grandmother who was charged with watching over me.

It took me a few days to decide to visit our priest, Father Maloney. People believe in the cathartic use of that. I'd never felt the need. Maybe, maybe though, they were right…

⁓⁓⁓

Edith King might have been born timid. Or maybe great timidity was an affliction caused in some way by her childhood. Who has solved the chicken and egg story of human existence about heredity and environment, as if in the end one or the other determined things? Jimmy never spoke about his mother's growing up. He didn't speak of her very much at all, as if her self-effacing timidity in a way transformed itself into a lack of presence in his thoughts. Anyway wherever you are in life, how does it matter how you got there, when you're pretty much who you are? Explanations, rationalizations take you backward to the unchangeable. What good? I am interrogating Freud's ghost. I am stepping on his toes. To what active good? I'm sure I'm ignorant doing that, so forget that I raised the issue.

In the end what is certain is that we are what we do.

In my mind I tell myself: look forward not backward, as I try now to write what mattered, with my motto borrowed from William of Orange, who founded a nation. No need to hope to set forth, no need for success to continue. And yet, okay, all I've been moved to tell you is the past. Because the past, after all, no matter where we go forward is there like a Doppelgänger. And if all the same I am trying to make the past my servant, to serve me as I type a way into a future? I go on with what Jimmy had once recounted:

Edith was a meek person. The world might well be a better place if the meek had more strength to act than they have, because the meek are more troubled by goodness, less driven to overriding self-assertion than the strong, but they don't. And they do not shape events. James King Sr. was a strong person.

And a handsome man in his Marine uniform, even the khaki one, when hers and his story became their future with a dance. The Cakewalk? The Castle Walk? The Foxtrot? Imagine this couple doing each and maybe all of them while James King literally swept Edith Cannon off her feet. On a night in 1917, when Spring weather in the South was making its deceptive case for a beneficent world. A colored band was playing Ragtime, the syncopated beat of the era. All the rage. You can think of that hiccup now as an intuitive embodiment of an apprehension in the air, a holding back against where the world was driving everyone that July. You can speculate on how that expression fit the times, and it might indeed have been truly so, as collective impulses realize themselves in what we all do. Yes, and I can imagine James King Sr. dancing. Hard to envision him doing that since, although, his nature softer then, he could have become a man who waltzed. They were young then, privileged enough, with his youth yet to play out. Or King might have been driven to dance and seize romance and love so as to block out an understandable queasiness over the great dance of death in which he was heading to become a performer. He was young while death, for him at that age, was not a vague possibility. It spread the flavor of importance onto many things.

Confederate Jasmine was a heady, growing presence in the precociously warm, moist air outside the Dumfries United Methodist Church in Dumfries, Virginia, that evening. Marines from the base twelve miles nearby were being honored for their will to heroism and treated to a social evening with some of the lovely young parishioners.

Edith Cannon was a pretty girl among them. She was very shy, but with a heart dedicated to good actions. She was not unfeeling in response to a handsome man's compliments. I could go so far to say vulnerable as self-effacing women are.

They all danced. The robust men sweated at least faintly in their tight uniforms, while the discreet perfume of the girls made up for that.

What was said between those two? What put them together when everyone else in the room was sampling the wares, so to speak, changing partners. From that night on, Edith and James saw each other over and over. Movies. Dinners. And then he had to sail away, but by then there was a real bond between them. She prayed that he'd survive his noble ordeal. And come back. And he did. Changed. Scarred, yes, but he'd reached the change that saved him from forever being crippled in his mind. He came closer to her within his faith. He went on to seminary and, right after they married, to a parish up North. And he remained as forceful and strong in his religious convictions as he'd been a powerful Marine. Which left Edith, who'd been an accommodating secretary in a real estate office, daughter of a homemaker and a carpet salesman, where?

She became a diligent wife—a pastor's careful wife with its role in his parish of a modest version of diplomacy. Always acting in deference to the pastor.

They had one child and he was Jimmy. She must have been a positively formative presence in his growing up: Jimmy became a brilliant scholar, an athlete, and the most popular person in his high school. He told me how grateful he was when she'd given him his dog Moe. The one other moment between them that stands out in my mind is the one after he'd come home from the hospital and his war. The day of the duck when she killed Moe…

She'd worried. Her husband kept saying it was not an infrequent sick thing: it happened to soldiers. It would take time for him to get over it, and she gave up talking about it to James, giving in to his wisdom, as she always, in any case, gave in to his opinions. She liked to call the pastor, to herself, her benevolent dictator, even though dictator was not a pleasant word for the times. But Jimmy was definitely deeply disturbed. That morning, as he'd begun to do, he stayed in bed late, not even sleeping, but when she would look in discreetly, she'd see him staring at the ceiling. At night, she could hear from the King's nearby bedroom, bursts of confused cries coming from him.

After a while he'd get up and be as normal as anyone. King said it was apparent that he'd been touched by "shell shock," but he was functioning, thank God, and not in a crippled state. The pastor had seen shell shock. There'd been those who became like vegetables afterward and those, with calm and rest, get over it. His son hadn't become a vegetable. He allowed that it was in his brave King nature not to.

Through a crack in the closed doorway of his bedroom, she saw him staring again. Whatever name James might give it; she saw a great depth of sadness. She shivered to think where that might take him and her mind brought back the imageless but brutal thought of her sister drowning.

His Europe had been a nightmare, but she would try to bring to mind the other side of it, which soldiers coming home had talked about with pleasure. He'd been in France. Paris, a beautiful city she knew she'd never visit but she'd seen pictures of it, intact through all the destruction of that war. The loveliest city in the world. Jimmy never talked about France, but once he had said, with a note of irony that the Germans had a saying: "to live like God himself in France."

He was home, her son was here, home. Edith decided to make a festive dinner for the family, around a French recipe, duck à l'orange. It was in one of her cookbooks. You didn't have to be a star chef to follow it well. A liquor store on Linden Boulevard would have a little bottle of Grand Marnier liqueur. What mattered first of all was the duck. The best duck would make all the difference. Not a Bohack's supermarket duck.

A real duck straight from the farm, and that was a kind of ace in the hole for her, because on Dutch Broadway, where Nassau County began, ten minutes away by car, stood one of the two survivors of the farms that were there before the developers took over that land. Just a few yards beyond the city line, opposite to where an eighteenth century white farmhouse had been destroyed for a gas station. Elmont Dairy with milk straight from the cow. The other, The Wallace Poultry Farm with its chickens and ducks strutting around near where cars went by. Not cooped up in some farm that was really a factory.

She got in the car at the head of the driveway. James would be back for dinner from a conference of Methodist ministers in Princeton, New Jersey. She'd driven him to the Long Island Railroad Station in Jamaica for him to get to Penn Station the day before, and she had the car.

She put the car in reverse. She heard a chilling screech. It wasn't until she'd pulled the car forward that she saw Moe lying there and trembling.

Jimmy ran out in his bathrobe. He threw on some clothes and drove with her to the vet in Springfield Gardens, nearby. She tried to say something. She hadn't known that Moe would wander out of his doghouse at the end of the drive. She hit him when he was coming back from what must have been an agreeable excursion, an amorous encounter. Jimmy was silent...his mood had become frozen.

In the veterinarian's second room, mother and son stared at the dog on the white Formica table, too weak now to make a sound out of the mouth that dripped blood. His belly and ribs had become concave.

"All I can do is put him out of his misery," the doctor said.

They didn't wait to see Moe die. They left him with the doctor, after Edith bent to kiss him on the head, to which there was no response. Each of them hadn't the heart to take home a corpse. There was no thought of sugaring over grief with a ceremony at a dog cemetery. They sat in the car before she could start it up to head, you can even say, to a new part of her life, because Moe was there, a part of the story she'd lived through during Jimmy's growing up. They sat together in the car, and Jimmy at last uttered something. It wasn't a word. It was a kind of whelp, almost an echo of Moe, that nearly frightened her. And then his chest heaved as he wept and she put her arms around him, a mother holding her child, and they wept together.

I think that moment he wept brought him back home and

brought him out of the world inside him, and maybe that was—as accidents can change things drastically—an ironic version of the achievement Edith had hoped for in her simplicity. Good, gentle Edith.

Love was in the air there, pure love, and he might have felt that—he told me the story not once. In the air like a visiting angel.

I was not there, but my imagination of that moment came to me with a vividness like a glow. But then I couldn't keep back a thought devoid of any image but a visceral presence of dread—a muddled awareness of an intense emotion's flipside of violence.

EIGHT

hadn't been to church since Easter two years earlier. My grandma went regularly, but she never forced me to accompany her. Maybe this was something like a Protestant strain in her piety: Everyone had to work out his own salvation. Maybe she lived with the conviction that there was room in this world for doubters, because willing to believe—fervently even—didn't endow the world with certain meaning. Maybe this uncertainty was also something He willed, with his veiled reasons, to be ever-present in our thoughts. To overcome it with our free will to choose devotion.

Father Maloney was not a priest with a simple faith either. I remember his coming to see Dr. Franklin. They saw each other often. Maloney had diabetes. If you were a friend of Alex Franklin, you would, like Cato Lyons, have to be fond of literature. The two of them, Franklin with his bad kidneys, Maloney with his pancreas, the atheist and the man of the cloth: drinking coffee, talking poetry, like Lyons and Franklin talking novels. Maloney would smoke many cigarettes, and I'd have to Airwick the room afterward. The priest conceded a fondness for the voice of Auden, Franklin's fellow atheist, while the doctor liked to recite the sputtered lyricism of Father Gerard Manley Hopkins (who was also a paradoxical classroom favorite of the dialectical materialist Sanford Rose.). They both loved poetry because it was "beautiful." You might have expected that their places in life would have meant reversed favorite poets, but their moments with their ailments together were perhaps even a time out from their opposing convictions. The priest and the doctor, two esthetes, then, for whom we could suppose that—with all each had to be concerned about over the woe in the world—beauty was indisputable truth. Maloney, knowing about Franklin's martyred Berlin relatives, avoided talking about the War. Father Maloney had returned from the Pacific, after he'd come near death himself, giving last rites to a soldier when a mortar struck again near them. His developing diabetes clinched his never going back to the battlefields.

They talked about fly fishing. Maloney kept and ate his trout, and Franklin did catch and release. I don't know why, one-time Maloney talked about his past. Coming in with a dish of fig newtons, I saw him take off the gloves he always wore. People may have said that they belonged somehow to his ecclesiastic costume, but the hands that he exposed were scarred all over.

"In the Jewish religion, I believe, Doctor," I heard him say, "a man who survives a deadly fire is someone who has been granted a miracle and bestowed with the touch of holiness. The French word for him is a *miraculé*. I have no reason to believe that second gift, but maybe you are looking at a man spared by God. And doubly. I am not in a position to know why."

"Doubly?" Franklin had an objective tone other than curiosity in his question. The interrogative pent of a man of science. Maloney was making a case for something to prove. Giving evidence.

"I'll tell you. I'm a son of a whore to begin with, Doctor, and that's not a metaphor."

He gave an apologetic glance at me—I was bringing more hot coffee—while his eyes seemed to say that that was not for my ears. I blushed, and left, but I couldn't keep myself from keeping the kitchen door open:

"There is a street in Nazareth, North Carolina, outside Raleigh, people call 'Cry Baby Lane.' Folks have been known to still hear children screaming there and to smell smoke. That much I can't believe, but I'll tell you why they think so.

"Son of a whore knifed by a client, dead before she could get last rites, I entered the orphanage of Father Price on what they call now 'Cry Baby Lane.'

I survived the famous fire there, jumping out a window. Nine-teen-o-five. I was fifteen. I pushed a quivering priest out a window before I jumped. He fell the wrong way and died. I survived. *Miraculé,* as the French put it.

"His orphanage in ashes, Father Price went off to preach his untarnished faith to the Chinese, and would die among them—of a ruptured appendix treated with herbs. His heart was buried beside Saint Bernadette in Nevers, France. Father Price is known to have written 3,087 letters to the Blessed Virgin Mary in his diary. Nothing, of course, is written about how they were addressed nor his getting replies. Maybe there was something else to learn in his faith: how exactly to post that mail. I am making fun of my own conscience, Doctor, just the two of us here in this room. Doubt is not a sin, going forward all the same is a virtue. Job is the Doppel-gänger in all our souls. But of course there's no empirical proof that there are souls. Nor that anything empirical matters in the end more than faith."

And me, in earshot as he went on.

"Add to this, Doctor: do not be the one to throw the first stone."

"The few of us kids who got out slept on the floor of a Catholic high school gym while they began getting people to take us, one by one. Which is how my name is Maloney. Katherine Maloney came down from Detroit when she'd read about the disaster, and I must have been a charming teenager because she went home with me. Bless her departed soul, and I mean that with emphasis; she was a widow, but she had a companion, Moira, and they shared a bedroom and they shared a bed. This said and observed, nothing shook my knowing that they were touched with the spirit of devotion that inspired my calling. They sent me to Catholic high school where I became who I am, and on to seminary, and my beloved two parents so to speak wept tears of joy at my taking the vows. The world the Lord has made is an intricate and—to say the least—mysterious place, but all things said, I trust Him on the job He has done. Who else has given us both to know morality and forgiveness for our shortcomings? Our consciousness endowed with conscience as if anointed by nobility?"

I didn't understand everything about Father Maloney, but I believed, in my state of distress—and yes guilt—that he was someone very understanding to go to, even if he'd say that I was two years late. But I didn't think that he would.

❧

I waited on a bench in the playground across the street from Sacred Heart. I thought that people who came to confess every morning would suspect something, seeing me among them, whom they hadn't in memory seen before. I watched them file out, one by one, having deposited their little wrongdoings—"I yelled at the kids" and such—their small ordeals of catharsis that paid for a soothing sureness about the why of the world. I especially didn't want to run into Wanda Nowak, whose noted piety dates beyond her coming over from Poland before the war. Piety had nothing to do with her being a gossip. I saw her cross herself once again in the doorway of the church, an extra effort that might have meant she had something of extra seriousness to confess that morning. I talk condescendingly now, but after all, you never know what is said in those booths—how awful things can indeed go on in a quiet place like Cambria. After all, every now and then, in the *Long Island Press*, you would read about someone poisoning her husband, or vice versa.

꧁

There was a smell of trapped air and the spice of incense. The empty church—built by the diocese before the Crash, when residents of a new place were grateful to add this presence of the neo-gothic, this historical anchor of credence, to our "Tudor" community. It echoed with the sound of a broom on the stone floor. Salvatore Flores, the gimp-legged sexton, a widower in his eighties, was sweeping. Flores was slow-witted; he didn't understand English well, though he'd emigrated from Sicily a quarter of a century ago. The church and his job in it were his haven from the uncertainties of a world in which he'd survived at the edge of destitution, shining shoes at a Greyhound Bus terminal. It might have been all the same better than poverty in Sicily.

Father Maloney was not in sight. I stepped into the confession booth and touched a little buzzer. I smelled the strong presence of tobacco smoke embedded in his clothing as he stepped into his side of the booth. Father Maloney, a heavy smoker, was not your serene priest.

He coughed, and stirred the air we were enclosed in, sending more of the evidence of his addiction my way. I heard the limping sound of Salvatore Flores' feet, as he kept sweeping. I took the plunge:

"Bless me father for I have sinned. It has been—Dear God, I don't know how long since my last confession."

"Two years, I would guess," he said.

"It has been two years since my last confession."

He coughed hard again. I wondered suddenly whether Father Maloney was sick, and it was as if the pity that came with that thought put me on a path toward my absolution.

"Yes," he said. "Yes?"

I got it out. I don't know whether he saw my tears through the grill. "I have committed…fornication."

I heard him shift for comfort. My eye was drawn to the purple of his stole, through the grill.

He waited a long time before he said:

"How old are you, Erin?"

That question wasn't in the ritual.

"Seventeen, eighteen in September, father."

I think I heard him say, under his breath, "Dear Jesus," and that wasn't in the ritual.

"Repeatedly?"

"Once."

"With consent?"

"Without resisting."

I burst into loud tears.

"Father, I felt sorry for him." Not the whole truth.

Salvatore may have heard my sobs. The sweeping stopped. I wondered whether the widower Flores had people close to him, whom he might favor with what he heard and saw in church.

"I feel sorry for you. So do you love him?"

"I'm not sure that I know what that is."

"When you love you know. It gets defined in how you act. I have to assign you a penance."

"Yes, father."

"If you don't love him, don't see him again."

"That will be my penance?"

"Yes. Repeat after me:

"Oh my God,"

"Oh my God."

"I am heartily sorry for having offended Thee."

"I am heartily sorry for having offended Thee."

"And I detest all my sins,

Because I fear the loss of heaven

And the pains of hell."

"Because I fear the loss of heaven…and the pains of hell."

"But most of all because they offend Thee, my God."

"But most of all because they offend Thee, my God."

He coughed again.

"Dominus noster Jesus Christus te absolvat," he said, and went on in Latin. My mind was drawn to realize that he had a southern accent. I'd never been to North Carolina. So I'd wandered from the importance of what was being said. I was thinking of that sad, middle-aged man, his cough, and not of me. Maybe that was indeed part of earning my absolution. I left. Should I have said thank you? I was late for my job at Dr. Lyons' place. I felt only somewhat better. I realized how weak my faith remained, and I hadn't really determined to do the penance Father Maloney had prescribed, which wasn't penance really but advice I should have heeded. Which would have left me nowhere. As I drove my bike in the street behind the church, I saw Father Maloney at the rear door, lighting up a cigarette. Wearing his black gloves.

"Your mother's coming home!" my grandmother said. That was the first thing she said as I went into the kitchen, where she was sitting at the breakfast nook with two little crystal cordial glasses and a bottle of crème de menthe. She poured and we toasted like regular drinkers. It was the bottle that she'd buy at Christmas time to last her a year. Her life wasn't rich in occasions for a toast, but this was definitely one. "My daughter's coming home, God bless her."

I kissed her on the cheek, inhaling her indescribable good smell, like a materialization of her nature. I was struck by a moment of panic: "Is Mom all right?"

"She's being discharged. Safe and sound. She's on her way to San Diego, USA, to finish her tour there. With luck, she'll be home for your eighteenth birthday."

Grandma was in her bathrobe. Before she'd received the telegram, she'd got ready for another night of ritual: a warm bath, silent prayers, getting ready to ease her worry in sleep. She shifted thoughts:

"This fellow, Jimmy King?"

"He's nice."

"What does his father think of mackerel snappers?"

"I don't know. We're not going steady, Grandma."

"And if he asked?"

"He's nice is all it is."

"And that's all?"

"Why are you interrogating me?" A second after I said it, I regretted taking that tone with her.

"I think of your future."

"My future." I sounded petulant again. How long could I hold back, counting the days.

"Your scholarship. Whatever you have planned. Your life. Don't tie yourself down now, Erin You're not made for a kitchen in Levittown or wherever."

She looked at my bleak face. "Something happened," I said.

"Are you pregnant?" she asked without a hesitation.

I was silent for a long moment. I looked down, counting again, this time the cherries on the oilcloth covering the kitchen table.

"I don't know," I answered. For the first time that question lurking in the dark of my mind was out in the light. "I might be," I finally got out.

"Dear God," my grandmother said, "Dear God." She said it lowly, not with anger nor shock.

"I did something horrible!"

My grandmother got up and walked to the kitchen cabinets. She opened one and there was another bottle. Whiskey. I'd never seen her whisky bottle before, but now she poured us each a drink to the brim of her little cut glass glasses. We didn't toast but we both gulped the whiskey down like a couple of Russians.

"We'll have to see," my Grandmother said.

"Let me scramble some eggs, Erin."

She turned from the refrigerator where she found the eggs.

"We'll see what we'll see," she said,

Not a word of reproof. I bless her forever.

Time went by, and we saw.

NINE

What everyone in Cambria had feared at last happened. It was among us. The plague that had reached elsewhere in Queens that we'd read about came to our happy land. The fourteen-year-old son of Leonard Liu, the owner of the Canton Palace was taken away to Mary Immaculate Hospital.

People were particularly panicked, because the twenty-five-cent luncheon at the Canton Palace was very popular. Mothers who shopped on Linden Boulevard would share their chop suey with their kids, and, although it used to be a joke to speculate over what otherwise uneatable Mr. Liu put in his undeniably tasty dish, people were frightened over whether terrible germs were part of the ingredients.

Liu closed his restaurant. It had been the great achievement in his life. His father had slipped through the Exclusion Act of 1882 with his own father, a "paper son" of Chinese already in San Francisco. He grew up in his father's laundry, in the Bronx, where he'd worked sixteen hours a day in a place the size of a bedroom. He and his mother, and Liu from childhood on, had labored there and saved money so that Liu could own a restaurant. Liu's own son was a brilliant student who would rise higher. Liu's son was fighting for his life now in an iron lung. Father Maloney, his regular patron, knew the whole pathetic story.

Dr. Mildred Smallwood, with the cancelled prom behind us, reacted by cancelling the weekly assembly at Jackson, so as not to be responsible for any large meetings not absolutely necessary.

We were kept in our homerooms to study instead. The graduation ceremonies were ahead, and logic said that if you ban assemblies of students, what sense does it make to fill the auditorium even more with parents, relatives, and neighbors? The principal called Cato Lyons to her office for another opinion. He simply said:

"I don't have any new answer, Mildred. Nobody does."

She went to the Student Council of the graduating class. I was there. It was kind of pathetic to see the strong-willed woman whom we knew hanging fire about a decision that might lie on her conscience as well as stain her career. But a graduation was a cherished milestone in our lives. We helped her out. Someone called for a vote, and the graduation ceremonies were voted down. We'd presented that as a recommendation. She was visibly grateful.

So there were no graduation exercises. The valedictorian speech I'd been writing and rewriting was to appear in *The Hickory Log*, the school newspaper. I was nervous about getting up there on the stage anyway.

Looking back, it seems like we took a big decision so easily in our stride. But the war, and the names of boys who'd been killed that would appear every Thursday in the *Press* with their cheerful photographs had made us used to far direr turns of events.

And so, what happened with our being graduated also turned out to be a positive thing. Over several days, in alphabetical order, each member of the senior class and her or his parents were called to Dr. Smallwood's office to receive a diploma. The principal turned out to be remarkable in turning things into a truly memorable experience. Meeting with the teachers, she'd boned up on knowledge of each student that allowed her to say something personal. Parents were amazed. She created a moment of unforgettable history in each of our lives.

I remember my turn. I was there with my grandmother. I'd bought her an orchid at Quigley's, with some of Dr. Lyons' pay. She'd been very disappointed about not hearing me give the speech that I'd been rehearsing for days. She'd pinned the flower to the jacket of a seersucker suit I hadn't seen her wear before. She'd especially gone to Gertz, in Jamaica, to buy it.

Sanford Rose came in the office without a greeting. Dr. Smallwood gave him a smile of recognition on a face that looked ill at ease. He testified simply that I was one of the best students he had and that he'd think of me each time he passed the honor roll outside the principal's office, with my name in gold as the first one for the names that year.

"There's a big world outside of Cambria for you, Erin," he said. His voice was urgent, and it sounded to me suddenly like a serious counsel: You have to get out of here.

Once Victoria had told Grandma that her husband had been briefly to Spain and come home very quickly, wounded. An imagined sight stayed in my mind of a town totally destroyed. The name? Belchite.

Far from Cambria.

The thought struck me that Sanford Rose, with his world of literature and poetry and who had crossed an ocean to take part in a momentous war in history, might have felt, with all that, like an exile in Cambria Heights. In that moment, I felt an impulse of pity for my teacher.

Dr. Smallwood seemed to exhale as his presence left the room. He went on to teach his next class.

She took up her own mission:

"It's an honor for me to give this diploma to our valedictorian," Mildred Smallwood told Grandma. "What more need be said? You're going to go very far, Erin, I am certain of it. You're a wonderful writer."

I wasn't certain. Grandma beamed. Maybe she was.

Ellen Dolland was a classmate, whom we all called the privileged Miss Dolland—her father's junkyard had become a very prosperous scrap iron business during the war, and she was privileged as well by her resembling an actress called Sally Blane, since oblivious in the history of Hollywood. Ellen Dolland was unmoved by the cancelling of the prom. She had already programmed her own private commemoration of that milestone in her life before it would lead to a future on the screen. It coincided with her eighteenth birthday. Her party at home didn't qualify as a dangerous crowded gathering. Ellen had done a short list of her guests. Myself included.

She had read a bestseller called "The Fountainhead" that people were talking about a lot that summer, and she had been talking it up among us. For my part, I found the fiction a kind of shallow acting out of the author's "philosophy," in which I also found an echo of Nietzsche's superman story, and we know what kind of super persons drew their reasons for being from that. Nietzsche wound up totally crazy, but our Ellen was in full flower of demonstrably elite intelligence beyond her pleasing features.

I have to say that the lot of us who responded to her invitation—and I have to confess that people were reinforced in their self-esteem by it—were indeed a designated elite. Each of us had an oval pin with the colors of our school on it, white and green. It was the badge of a society called Arista. To get in to that elite circle, you needed a 90 average in your studies.

I was a member of Arista. I never heard of the possibility of turning down membership, and wasn't driven by a desire to do so. Arista is taken from the Greek, *aristos*—the best. What, I thought, could be wrong about being designated the best?

It fitted in any case very well into Ellen's ethos of elitism. The invitation for her birthday, also tied to graduation, went out to the selected.

Ellen was on her way to Radcliffe, and although she had the grades, her father was paying her way, an easier way in than a scholarship.

Her father's barbecue was exceptional. The best steaks. We ate them with relish and drank beer from a keg—her father overseeing our consumption—while we buried the thought that the beef might have been still black market.

The talk about what next, where the best were going and what they were going to accomplish, left me very uncomfortable. It was nighttime, and I made my way quietly with my dish of food toward the unlit edge of the backyard, where there was a glider. When I got there, Jimmy King was sitting in the dark.

Jimmy had been in Arista two years before all of us, which could be a reason for his being invited, but I knew that Ellen had a strong undeclared crush on him, of which he hadn't, as far as I knew, taken great notice. Now he was sitting alone on the glider.

He looked at me, drew me down onto the glider beside him, and did not let go of my hand. His hand was cold. We didn't speak for a long moment, while the elated chatter of the others reached us. Then he just said:

"Forgive me, Erin."

I didn't have an answer. He said:

"You know what I mean."

I still couldn't answer. I was very sorry. I was so sorry that what had happened was as if a stranger had forced his way into our story, and had paradoxically violated the special intimacy between us. Like a fabric ripped apart.

The thought came to me of what Ellen's favorite author had written: "To say I love you one must first know how to say the I."

Who was the "I" I thought I was? I was a bundle of conjectures about life and where I was in it. That wasn't a foothold for drawing someone close to me from outside my history of pure family love. I hadn't become a full person. And the author's other facile maxim came back to me to trouble me: "Pursue your own happiness as your highest moral aim." How could I?

Jimmy changed the subject, but didn't make things more cheerful. "I have a rendezvous," he said. The way he said it, choosing that non-colloquial, old expression, made it reverberate with portent. I thought of another damned soldier, Alan Seeger, and his "rendezvous with death." "With a comrade," he said, another word we never used. Maybe in his state, he was framing the meeting in importance with more formality than the colloquial. "We were together in the Division. He's got a piece of his leg that's metal now. He's in a bad place in his mind."

I didn't know what I might have answered, what might have been the good answer.

I told Jimmy I was going to get some iced tea. Where I was, in a larger sense going, where best?—I did not know, and I didn't have a popular philosopher to guide me. And Jimmy's "I?" Who he was, what he was now, with the glory in his yearbook behind him? Whatever could anyone do to help, to move him now from a dark place? The place in his mind. I see him sitting there far from the charcoal fire and the aroma of steak, from the festive string of lights overhead. His almost hidden blank face, a mask that didn't cover distress.

I felt for him, but the emotion stayed within me; it wasn't expressed. It was an emotion that Ellen Dolland's favorite author disdained. Empathy…which didn't make things feel any better for me. My I. In any case, I didn't bring myself to break the fact to him *that I was late.*

⚜

And things would get worse.

I made my way into the kitchen to say goodnight and thanks to Ellen, telling her again happy birthday. She held onto my hand. I was never a close friend of hers, but what she said confirmed my opinion of her. She was privileged; her family had money. She was bright and bright enough to get into Radcliffe. I have to say that my being at the head of the class made me an acquisition of worth, a sort of prize in her selective acquaintances. Why else the gesture, to which I didn't say no? Why not? She said, "Erin, could I ask you a favor? I like the way you dress." I'd never given much attention to how I dressed. She went on, "I have to go into the City to get a wardrobe for going off to Radcliffe. Would you come with me? We'll have lunch at Larré and you'll just have to spend a little time at Lord & Taylor. We'll take my car. Did you see my new car for graduation?"

Saying no to her invitation would have sounded very unfriendly. I had no reason to say no. Fatefully, I said yes…

༄

Ellen and I set off, in the two-tone baby blue and white Nash convertible that her parents had given her for being graduated. The weather was good. She lit up an ivory-tipped cigarette and turned on WQXR to Beethoven. I really did feel good. She parked the car at some expensive garage and we were in time to be at Lord & Taylor for the ten-a.m. opening.

The sound system was playing light jazz, while salesgirls in white gloves were arranging folding chairs on the other side of the revolving doors. Women who had come in were invited to sit there, while a woman in a starched uniform stood beside a tea cart with demitasses on it. The jazz faded; an orchestra struck up the Star-Spangled Banner. The main doors opened, the people outside took the queue and came in. We drank a coffee and headed on the now moving escalator to the College Shop.

It was a new experience for me. I admit: Looking back at that peculiar ceremony of that luxurious store made a big impression. I felt uncontrollably diminished by it. I knew Ellen's world in Cambria, but this was another place on the landscape of her life.

I told Ellen I liked everything she chose. A lot of tweed and paisley blouses. A little black dress for special moments. She really looked good in it. With all else, Ellen was privileged by her good shape, her good blonde looks.

"Anything you like?" she asked. I said I thought she made very good choices.

"I mean personally."

"I have my whole outfit for college," I lied. "I have no more room in my luggage."

It was noon. We'd gone through her tryings-on.

She shrugged and we went on to Larré after she paid a lot of cash. She checked her Lord & Taylor shopping bags with the store. Those crisp white boxes, each with a big red rose on it, that people could identify. Badges of class. We'd come back after lunch. The garage was nearby.

"Let's walk," Ellen said. Lots of air. Manhattan. A bustling bright world. Store after store calling to you. This island was going to be my new home. For a moment, I felt oddly like I was leading her now.

"You know Larré?" she asked. I didn't. This was as far as my perverse sensation of leading lasted. We went inside and the headwaiter knew her. It was " Bonjour, Mademoiselle." And "Bonjour, Pierre."

It wasn't a fancy place, but she explained all the lore. Larré was authentic and very inexpensive. It was really French. We could even hear people speaking French as we went to our table. "You know who comes here? People you, Erin, would definitely relate to. Duchamp? A lot of artists, real French people like the ones we've just passed, who came over during the War."

We had my first real French lunch. Snails. Brains in black butter and capers, a custard called crème caramel. And we drank rosé wine, a glass each. The waiter didn't blink when Ellen ordered wine.

"If they know you here, they don't card you," she whispered. Anyhow I have indeed turned eighteen. You're my tolerated guest."

With that I learned that lunch was her treat. "After all the help you've given me," she said. At that point I wasn't going to embarrass myself with a protest. I had to take it that it was a dictate of an etiquette I was supposed to understand.

She lit another cigarette with our demitasses. Then she told me, and what had been an irresistibly pleasant day hit me like a rainstorm.

"I'll tell you," she said, "because you're such an intelligent person and aren't stuck in a lot of stuff that doesn't mean anything in the modern world. You know, about sex."

What could she have possibly have heard?

She said, "You're looking at an ex-virgin. Better sooner than later."

I didn't open my mouth. I was uncomfortable with her confession. Then she said:

"You know, Jimmy King. I've always had a crush on him. He's somebody."

She looked over at me, as if I were to envy her conquest. "We did it," she said. "He stayed to the very end of the party. My folks had gone to bed. He came in the kitchen to help me clean up. Next thing I know my skirt was up and my panties were down."

She looked for my reaction. I don't know what she read in the dismay on my face.

"Erin, you know, it's natural. It's nature. I feel liberated, like an initiation. Was it great?"

She'd expected me to ask that. I didn't.

"It was a bit rough. But. It was something!"

Right then a feeling of bitterness swept over me. Not of jealousy, but a sudden feeling that her "natural" was part of a judgment of life that made everything ordinary, and that there was nothing in the least profound in what I tried to comprehend about my own feelings. And so I couldn't even harbor blame—neither his nor mine. This was it. Life.

I'd never felt so contemptuous about the world we lived in before that moment at Larré. I've fought that impulse of contempt when it rose in me ever since. We drove home to WQXR again and she took my not talking as an example of my deep devotion to fine music.

❧

Jimmy sat on a bench facing the lake in Hempstead State Park for a long time. His friend, P.J., came up after a while on a bike, and when he pedaled Jimmy could see his metal calf. P.J. had suggested that they meet in a bar in Hempstead, but Jimmy wanted air and was fearful that the meeting might end with their both drowning their woes in whiskey. P.J. didn't have a car. He was having a hard time getting a little job. People pitied his leg, but worried about what could happen to him handling heavy things. P.J. had no education beyond the high school general course. Traveling with the war had opened horizons to him, and he'd paid dearly for that education, which he could put to no use. Nobody cared whether he could order a glass of wine in French or a beer in German.

He sat down beside Jimmy and began to chain smoke. His fingers were all yellow.

"You up to anything?" P.J. asked.

Jimmy looked out at the lake. An old Black man in a baggy dress suit was fishing. Here? An optimist, Jimmy thought. They exist. Did he also think that the suit made him feel better about himself? An old man with nothing to do but throw a line into some lake where maybe there were fish and believe the possibility of success.

"Kept me a Luger," P. J. said.

A rainbow-colored fish was flashing in the air. At the end of the guy's line. He'd indeed caught a sunfish.

"I figure we're owed," P.J. said. "And I can't even get a lousy job.

"Do they figure we're owed, Jimmy? Give me a break. It's like the way I am, I can have an accident on the job and they're in for a law suit."

Jimmy was beginning to feel that he'd made a mistake. The sight of the old man's luck had given him an irrational, positive moment in his thoughts, while P.J. was sending his mood into a deep descent. He had his demonic woes, but what were they compared to P.J.'s fake calf?

He said, "Do you have trouble sleeping?"

"I get angry," P.J. said.

"At what we saw?"

"What we saw? The world is one long latrine; what we saw was just some more evidence. Not to mention how we got there."

"I keep seeing the camp."

"I see the gas and electric bills at the end of the month, and a micro-pension…Well we did the job on those guys."

P.J.'s voice took on a new note of joy. Jimmy sensed that the evocation of violence properly accomplished had eased P.J.

"They were soiling their pants. After what they did to people who couldn't lift a finger."

"It wasn't the same guys."

"They were the same team, friend."

Jimmy saw the "job" again, vividly in his mind. The SS Garrison next to the camp. All but a few of the real guards had run away. P.J. set down a .50-caliber Browning and shot a dozen SS men, stretching it out. The others waited their turn. This was another piece of the world Jimmy had known.

It all came back, his bad dreams in daylight now. A bad idea this meeting.

Dead in piles in the courtyard, down to skeletons before they were killed. The freight yard had fifty cars on a train and every car was full of corpses. The living like ghosts...

"Maybe P.J. it helps to talk about...all that."

"Talk is cheap, friend."

P.J.'s "friend" was becoming irritating. He thought they were really friends. Been through it together, and now P.J. could make "friend" sound aggressive. Jimmy was now "the other" who didn't know what it was like to have been harmed by life the way he was.

"Do I sound resentful?" P.J. asked.

"If I were in your shoes," Jimmy began.

"What is that, a joke?"

"What are you going to do?"

"Hey, sometimes I think I'm going to clean up my Luger and walk into a filling station or a liquor store or whatever and say, come on, hand it over. You owe me. I am owed, my friend."

"Don't ever do that, P.J."

"But suppose I had to run out. How am I going to do that?"

The fisherman was walking away. What's he going to do with the one four-inch sunfish whose belly Jimmy saw flash again in the sun? He heard in his mind: Rainbow Division. The fisherman walked away.

They sat there totally alone now in silence.

"If you squeeze your bike in the back, I can drive you home," Jimmy said. "It's my father's car."

P.J. got up and got on his bike.

"Forget about it," he said, "I'm no invalid."

He pedaled away pretty fast.

"Jimbo!" P.J. called back to a friend again. "My ma will make us supper!" He lifted a hand from his handlebar and did a thumbs up. And that was all that was positive in Jimmy's meeting with P.J.

A week later, the front page of the *Long Island Press* had the story: Pasquale J. Santori, a decorated veteran from Hempstead, had put a German pistol in his mouth and blown his head away. And with that event, P. J. bequeathed Jimmy another nightmare for Jimmy's collection…

ॐ

It was the meeting Jimmy told me about after he'd come back from P.J.'s wake. I couldn't tell where his thoughts were or the trajectory of where his mind was going. He said he needed to talk about the death of an old friend; could we just meet and talk? Meet and talk. I said okay; could I have said no? We sat on a bench near the Q4 bus stop. No place congenial, but congeniality wasn't in order.

P.J.'s widowed mother, he said, moved him by the dignity of her grief—although she couldn't look more devastated. She was a simple woman. P.J. had told him that she had immigrated to America with her husband, fleeing Mussolini. He was a stone mason and died of a frail heart working with heavy stones. P.J. was their only child, they didn't plan it that way, being devout Catholics. They didn't go further to know why, with the chance of one of them winding up with an onus like blame. Calabrians considered having big families to be respectable behavior; not having one brought on a mixture of pity and shamefulness, which she'd endured rather than casting blame on her husband.

There were enough collateral relatives there to fill the house. Maria Santori cooked an elaborate Calabrian meal, served with wine and then anisette. P.J., Jimmy said, would have been cheered by all that.

"She came up to me when everyone was into family stories and I was standing in a corner of the dining room alone. She was grateful that a friend of P.J.'s was there. I didn't see any other one. When last I saw him, as I told you, he was not, well, amicable.

"She wanted to show me what was left of him, the things around him that in a way defined him. We went upstairs to his room. A little bedroom with a desk along with a chest of drawers and a bed. There was not much to show, but I think she took me to see what the suicide could not tarnish, what he and she were both proud of.

"P.J. had told her that I was a swimmer, and she thought it touching to show me a concrete, lasting presence of a bond in our friendship, two great athletes.

"On the chest was a big silver trophy cup. He'd won it while at Hempstead High. P.J. Santori had been the champion 100-yard runner on all of Long Island. The way she said it, it sounded like Long Island was a vast country.

"She was a simple woman, Erin, but did what she had to do. It was a respectable wake, and I don't know who she saw to get a dispensation to get P.J. buried in a Catholic cemetery. Who in the church, who in their community who had a line to the church? Anyway…"

I said I thought that Father Maloney, if it was his parish, would have done that for an invalid war hero. Jimmy shrugged. He didn't know Maloney as I, unfortunately, had come to know him, and I could not yet bring myself to tell him why.

❧

"My dog got killed, Doctor", Jimmy said.

Lyons looked at him. It was the first thing Jimmy said when he came to the appointment.

"It was the icing on the cake," Jimmy said.

"You're here about the death of your dog?"

"You don't look so hot, Doctor."

Lyons looked at him again.

"I'm here because I don't know. I can't sleep. Everything—

it's like there's no sun anymore. I'm here because you're a doctor, Cato. I had doctors over there. They didn't help. Sent me off into the wide world. It's like you can't see anything straight, like a dread. My friend died too, P.J. blew his brains out with a souvenir Luger. Well it was mind over body in his case; he told himself what he needed. I have a problem with mind over body. My body won't sleep. My mind can't talk it into it. Nightmares."

Jimmy got up and walked to the window, with his back to Lyons. As if he'd stepped away from his confession. Lyons sensed his anguish, the pain and the pain of showing it. But as he turned around Jimmy's eyes were imploring. All the doctor could say was: "I don't know what I could do," and it hurt him to confess another example of his own incapacity.

"Pills, doctor?"

"They won't change things. Not any I know. They'll get you hooked. And then without them it will be worse."

Jimmy shook his head and shrugged. Hopelessness settled over him. He reached out of his private darkness:

"You don't look so hot yourself, Cato."

"You came about you. I'm sorry I couldn't say more than I said."

Jimmy was still standing in front of the doctor's desk, the object that was in some way like a throne, the seat of ministering. "I read about all the kids. The sickness. You must feel very bad, very…hopeless."

Jimmy wasn't leaving. The moment had turned from professional to intimate, and Lyons was all the more discomforted.

Jimmy's reaching out from himself had pushed it that way. Cato was without cover now. He found a package of cigarettes in a drawer. Jimmy saw it and shook his head, with a look that discerned a paltry gesture.

Lyons got up with no next move. He lit his cigarette and reached behind a row of medical books. He came back with a bottle.

There were paper cups in a package on a table behind his desk. He put two down and poured scotch.

"To your health," Cato said.

Jimmy raised his cup. "Yours too."

Cato said. "After what we've lived through, say thanks." He didn't sound convincing. "Right, the kids. You watch them suffer. You watch them die. A spectator."

They drank. Said nothing. Cato refilled their paper cups. He drank hurriedly and Jimmy took the cue.

"There's a room full of sickness waiting on the other side of the door; what more can I tell you, Jimmy?"

"Stay well, doctor," Jimmy said. He took Cato's hand and shook it before he left. There was no question of a prescription or a payment. Nothing accomplished except a useless complicity.

⁓

"I had a conversation with Jimmy King."

Lyons' looked for my reaction as he took the cup of coffee that I was about to put on his desk.

"He's a very distressed young man, your friend.

"You'd mentioned him to me. Something about whether his— Jimmy's—distress that you saw could be helped."

He paused for me to say something. By then my look gave things away. And he perceived that.

"You two," he began…

Silence.

"Sit down and allow me to say something: I know you more than a little, I think, my sensitive 'Miss Efficiency.' I knew you before I inherited your kindness—from all that Dr. Franklin had told me."

"Are you in love?" he asked delicately now, as if the question weren't weighted with apprehension. I didn't answer but looked down now like a child being seriously scolded, and he took measure of the impact of what he'd said.

"Are you all right? How old are you?"

"I'm seventeen."

I couldn't muster an answer to the rest of what he'd asked. I just burst into tears. He raised my head to look up by holding me by the arms.

"And it went far." It wasn't said to me as a question.

He didn't prolong the excruciating moment of silence that followed. With which he'd had his confirmation.

"You've missed…?"

My silence again was his answer.

"No other problems with your health?"

"I'm going to have to have a specimen, Erin.

I knew what he meant. The undeniable verdict. The frog.

Three days later, the frog spoke.

The last thing Dr. Lyons said that day was, "We will have to think hard about this…"

꧁

I thought about it. Nights when I couldn't sleep, my chest covered with sweat each morning. When I couldn't bring on the escape of sleep, I spent the late hours trying to imagine who I would become next. I'd had a plan. I'd be eighteen and what followed. Barnard. To write, and I'd resolved to take on the risk of failure at that. That was my blueprint, but it was about me, and now I was more than just me.

So what could I imagine? College forsaken. For us both. Marriage? And what would he do, when we're chained by fate to each other? And I knew I could no longer trust him to be a messenger of happiness. Not to me—and a child?

I heard Sanford Rose reading John Donne to us: "No man is an island." All lives in this hazardous world intertwine; I understood that viscerally. Where does morally provoked bonding become bondage? What do we owe whom, when, and where with all that? I felt uncertainty tied to dread. I got out of bed, a morning after several of those sleepless nights. I had to do something to think of something else and I remembered that it was a morning, with school over, for Victoria Rose's dancing class.

꿁

My body ached as if it were punishing itself. Deliberately punishing me. Stomach cramps. Spiraling, on the dance floor, I couldn't get back from feeling twisted and my falls thudded like tumbling—like from out of a window. Victoria kept eyeing me, but she didn't for some reason hold me up as an example to correct—as if beyond the impulse of a teacher, she sensed that something other than my body movements had gone wrong, and making an example of them to everyone could be more serious than embarrassing.

We got though the exercises. It was the last lesson of the season. School was over and Sanford wouldn't have to teach until the fall. They were going up for the rest of the summer to her father's house in Massachusetts, where she'd see her mentor, the renowned Martha Graham, and watch her dance at Jacob's Pillow.

The others filed out; some kissed her cheek goodbye. Our number had been winnowed to a few faithful to her, after the others' families had faulted Rose for his housing Porter. As they left the new storefront studio, Victoria held me back with a hand on my shoulder.

"I'll miss you, Erin," she said, but you're going beyond my little class to become someone who matters for the good in the world out there. I know that. It's Barnard?"

I nodded. My pelvis was beginning to cramp again.

"I know you have the grace, and Sanford knows you have the brains."

She held my arm and looked into my face, as if she could pierce my distress, and without prying into it, which she must have felt I wasn't ready for, she said something sincere and comforting. She gave me the gift of a confidence.

"Can I say I think of you like the daughter I didn't have, Erin? When you decide to be a dancer, you don't have children. It changes the body, and it takes you away from the dedication it needs to be able to be a dancer."

She looked at me silently a long moment, and ever since I've wondered if somehow signals had crossed and she'd seen into my particular distress. I lowered my eyes. She kissed my cheek. Nothing more was said. Not ever.

TEN

My mother had come home changed. They'd sent her for her discharge to the Saint Albans Naval Hospital, where she'd gone through a "work-up," as the doctors called it. Her health hadn't shown any harm, but the tense years were there in lines on her face.

We were sitting with my grandma over coffee in the hospital cafeteria. The room was filled with men in bathrobes and bandages, talking to their loved ones in hushed voices, the torment over what they'd gone through and survived seemed to seep out of their hesitant conversations. We realized how, in this room, *we* were lucky ones, while the absence of my father at our family reunion brought back a darker solemnity.

The day the three of us—my parents and I—went to the Long Island railroad station came back to me. The train took him out of our lives, while we watched him disappear from a windy platform.

There we were now, sitting amid the Formica tables, in a banal, bland room that all the same was full—charged with eventfulness. It was a place embodying a moment in history that had raised us, all of us there, from our banalities, and had marked us with the revelatory power of calamity, transformed us with meaning about what mattered, things we'd never thought and certainly not dreamed would ever season our lives.

Grandma looked at me, and her look said, "Don't ask." Don't ask about what mother had gone through. Everything that mattered now was in the future. I didn't ask, and so our conversation was banally full of affection.

I remembered her letter after her arriving in Hawaii. She was "all right" and working in a hospital with a lot of wounded soldiers. Among them there were still many who'd been brought in from Pearl Harbor. Did she have unbelievable hope that her husband—who was at the bottom of the bay—would turn up in an ambulance one day? And then there was nothing but bland, small mentions after that. When her letters didn't come, I took her silence as evidence of her abandoning me. I was thirteen with an adolescent's narrow understanding of what was going on in the world she was born into.

A lot of women volunteered to be nurses after Pearl Harbor, and they were sent to training centers to learn as quickly as possible what they had to know to minister to the wounded. Nurses with experience were rare in the Pacific and the Japanese were giving them a harvest of horror to reap. My mother was a registered nurse, and they shipped her right away to Fort Shafter. On arriving, she wrote that the island of Oahu looked like paradise and the nurses' quarters were sheer comfort. There came few letters after that. Then none…

Mother came home from Saint Albans hospital that night, and before she went to bed—right after eating supper and while she said goodnight—she held out an unsent letter.

"You know, there were times when I grieved with the thought that you may have felt I forgot you in giving myself to all that was so important. I wanted to protect you from the distress of what I lived through—day in and day out, still not knowing how it would end. Whether we'd awake from that nightmare. But I saved this. It's my life."

I've saved the letter she gave me, that she'd never sent.

It was dated March 8, 1942:

"There is a bizarre and shocking contrast in our lives. Hawaii is gorgeous, the nature, the halcyon weather, and the amenities for the army and the nurses that were created here before the war are idyllic, although personally I don't profit from the social life, which in any case has taken on a pall. Some of the women still drink with the officers at their club, but there are fewer and fewer of those left, and the dances where some of the women would go to find romance have been cancelled.

"But Waikiki Beach is spectacularly beautiful, the miles of sand with palms behind, overlooking a clear blue sea. I go there swimming with some of the girls when we have a respite, but that's becoming very rare.

"We work from early morning until late at night when the casualties arrive from the islands and lie on the floor where there is room. Our hospital at Fort Shafter has only 450 beds, and we're not pressed to see them emptied by letting someone die. Medicine and antiseptics are rare and the surgeons are operating in a hurry from one patient to another with their bare hands. We're thankful that our store of anesthesia has not run out, or we would be in a nightmare daily—as if in the Civil War.

"They come here with every damage to a body possible.

"The burn victims are the most horrifying—from the Japanese incendiary bombs We treat them with poultices of tannic acid or a bactericide with the name Triple Dye, and some doctors apply petroleum jelly or bicarbonate of soda. But it can all be of pitiful little use. Once the burns have reached the third degree, deep below the skin the complications are disastrous. Something in the burnt flesh creates poisons that attack the organs, so what happens inside the body is the worst effect. We drip-transfuse them with a variety of liquids—hit or miss on which are the most effective—to do fluid replacement, trying to keep the thickened blood caused by the burns from creating deadly clots. The doctors perform skin grafts that are sometimes very effective. The other night, I saw a surgeon deftly apply a skin graft to where eyelids were burnt away. The man died of the rest of his burns nonetheless.

"All and all I am here as if in a horror hospice for plague victims in the middle ages, but I am sustained by the dire need of my labors.

"The cost in human lives lost or destroyed gets more and more horrendous and I shudder to imagine how awful it will be when we're obliged to defeat the Japanese in their homeland.

"I say destroyed, and I mean in mind as well as body. One out of twelve of the wounded coming in are not visibly afflicted but radically hurt in the mind. It's called "combat fatigue" or they're "shell-shocked" and they're here, they're told, to get over it with rest and relaxation. But they stare endlessly into space or they shout at night, having nightmares where they're reliving the horror of combat—a lot of it hand to hand. They get violently angry and start fights with the staff and doctors. Some of them have to be restrained. They give them shock treatments where they put electrodes to their temples while they lay strapped down with a towel in their mouths to keep them from swallowing their tongues when they become epileptic from the current. Some of them have an operation in their heads. It makes them no longer violent, but they walk around like zombies."

Did she wonder, seeing the horror of the burn victims, whether her Brian had died that way, before the Arizona went under? Did she have her nightmares of him enveloped in fire? As much as anyone, my mother deserved a Purple Heart for what the war had done to her. What right had I then, with all that, to be resentful over her willfully leaving—leaving her only child behind? I was thirteen years old, and already could perceive that her love for her husband had become the anchor of her life. I would have to bear with the burden of her loss, and take my share of her powerful love the way it came.

It was Grandma, who finally told me what my mother avoided telling me about after Hawaii. My mother was on a hospital ship, being rescued from one of her embattled war zones when it was bombed by Kamikaze pilots, and fished out of water. With the direst irony, she lived the how of her husband's death, as if in some mystic way she was willed to share that moment. My mother was what the French call entire—forever stricken, while so complete in her character that she lived her nature to the fullest. I'd have to take her love for me in all that, as it came.

⚜

For days on end, I had been living in a kind of denial, as people say these days. At times I was nauseated, but nothing else—except for the fateful absence—felt like a change, although my life's change was absolute and with it was installed the irrepressible question of one great open-ended future that I did my best to keep driving from my mind.

My mother sat me down beside Grandma. "You have your life ahead of you," she said. "Do you want to decide a way ahead of you now? To where? Does he know? Would he be ready to assume? If so, I don't see where it will be college for either of you, but it's your lives and this is the world as it is. I have to say that you alone have to know where you're going.

"If you have a child, you'll have to get married or live like a pariah, in the world as it is. Do you want to marry him, do you choose, above all else, your love—if you really know what that is?"

She waited for a beat of silence before she put it bluntly: "I didn't hear you say that you love him."

"Maybe it was in every way an accident," I said. "Maybe everything has been an accident, everything we knew before was, after all, as if we were just incidentally together. We thought we shared our intelligence but, looking back now, not who we each fully were. And then he shared the consequences of his affliction."

"You can't say willfully."

Had I sounded bitter and forgetful? I was stricken with resentfulness.

I finally got it out. "It seems, for him, there were...others."

I thought that I could see in her wet eyes that she loved me, but the calamity that had been her fate had given her a retaliatory reserve that was part of whatever vengeance. It came to facing suffering with dignity, I think, but with a wary coldness—as if...can it be so—everyone shared the guilt of being, as if belonging on a landscape of hostility, collaborating with a world that was, all told, hostile and disappointing. I would come to know the sorrow of having to realize that her personality harbored her unhealed wounds. Later in life, I would know a good friend in college who had a word for her boyfriend's mother that expressed that state of existence like no other word. It was Yiddish: *verbissen.* Bitten by a mad dog called fate.

I said to them both there at the kitchen table: "He doesn't know. I'm not going to tell him."

My mother said again that it was my decision; she would not urge me to choose what she would. As I sat there looking into space, she stood up and pulled me into her arms. And with that I realized that the urge to love was embedded in her as deeply as sorrow.

No one is one thing.

My decision. For the first time in my life, I had a decision so greatly consequential to make. I went up to my room and sat at my desk looking out the window at the cookie-cutter Tudor houses on 240th Street. I imagined a little "starter house" in Levittown or Valley Stream. In my mind I was already a refugee from there. I wept over my great mistake, and I wept being faced with the consequential decision. And I decided.

❧

My mother went to see Lyons by herself. I'd learn from my grandmother how it had gone.

She said, "Erin has asked me to speak to you about her dilemma."

"I know about it," he said.

"She's decided that she has to go forward with her life."

He listened with a look more grieved than pained.

"We've given great thought to what is right." And with that, she bet her whole hand. "Erin has the deepest respect for you as a human being. Please, do what is right."

There was a long silence between them. I think of them now, two deeply war-scarred human beings who'd battled calamity.

He said, "I need a week. I won't go into that. Give us a week."

For a week, Cato Lyons drank glassfuls of water and never a drop of alcohol. He woke up with a clear head and when he held out his hand, he was sure that it would be steady.

❧

When I saw Dr. Lyons again, she had been there ahead of me. She sat waiting, while I went into his examination room.

"Is it still true that you're going to Barnard?" he asked quietly, the first thing he said to me. He waited to hear my confirmation, but all that I could do was nod. My mother had watched me go to him and when I looked back, her face betrayed her stoicism. She'd seen enough worry over operations. I looked at the strange table where there were straps and stirrups he'd set up like an instrument of torture, and a chair with straps in Sing Sing came into my mind.

There was an undercurrent of grief that he'd all but hid as he went about his task. Miss Efficiency had added more distress to his life; it was like an act of disloyalty, but he said, gently, before he made the last gesture:

"Promise me, Erin," he said, "that you'll have the courage to make something very worthwhile of your life. There are too many dangerous crossroads in our world."

It was quick. I felt pain and bled. Dr. Lyons gave me a drug called penicillin, which had been used during the war and gone out to the public in March.

I was two weeks short of eighteen. I survived. I healed. I would go on to Barnard. He had broken the law—his oath?—for my future…

Then the big else happened.

Jacqueline Porter came to Dr. Lyons with a child in fever. Not much, not much more than a hundred, a state that children have easily, but mothers worry when a kid keeps crying and you don't know why.

Does she vomit? he asked. No. Did her limbs hurt or are they stiff? No. All noes. Did she seem to start to cry at the same time these past few days? Yes. Her eyes were watery. Her stomach seemed to him bloated. Did she seem all right when she wasn't in a fit of crying? Yes. Diarrhea? Yes. Sucked strongly at her bottle? Yes. Rejects her mother when she tries to hold her? Yes.

Lyons went through the symptoms of colic and sent Jacqueline and her daughter home. Make sure the hole in the nipple of her bottle isn't too large letting her suck in air, he said. Burp her after feeding. Keep her in a dark, quiet room.

"We have just one room," she told him.

He looked at her a moment, trying to have an image of what she described. "Do you have a fan?" he asked.

She had a fan.

"They sometimes like to listen to a gentle sound nearby. There is not much that you can immediately do to treat colic, but it cures itself."

Polio does not. The next day little Lorraine Porter was stiff all over and gasping for breath. An ambulance took her to Jamaica Hospital. She was too small for an iron lung. Her death was not a long ordeal. I'm moved to believe, given the dreadful and hopeless alternative for an infant, Dr. Lyons had hoped his way into a more encouraging diagnosis, hoping against hope that it would be right. I don't know what state Lyons was in. Even if Lyons had got his diagnosis right, it would not have mattered. Nothing really was effective. Some got through it, survived, recovered, and some did not. Infants had almost zero chance. I don't know how some children got over it, even impaired, while others didn't. I've never heard Father Maloney's view on the polio lottery.

❧

It was an off and on brilliant day outside when Jimmy came to see the Porters, but the light was all enfeebled when it came through the windows and white curtains of their place on basement windows above the knotty pine walls. The grayed light was a kind of chorus for their gloom, as Jacqueline and Warren greeted him in silence, in the basement where Warren Porter had wound up. It was, Jimmy noticed, all the same—neat, even in a way attractive. Rose, he knew, had finished the basement himself in knotty pine, with that stretch of rusticity to the walls that gave the single room below ground the consoling edge of a presence of the world of nature. The Porters' furnishings were simple, but attractive. Jacqueline invited him to sit in the "early American" armchair opposite the fold-out couch where they sat down—the place they slept. There wasn't much else there but a crib—empty except for a stuffed rabbit—which they both could not stop looking at, as if its companion in that crib would be there in her rightful place again.

Jacqueline made tea.

"A whisky, Jim," Warren said.

He took a bottle of bourbon from a built-in chest.

Jimmy hadn't even spoken yet. Couldn't get out what to say.

He didn't decline. Warren poured for the three of them. Neat.

Warren finally said, "She never cried, not until it really hurt."

Jacqueline drank down her bourbon and rushed to the bathroom.

"I don't get it," Jimmy said.

Porter looked at him curiously. "You mean?"

Jimmy shrugged.

The two men who'd come back from hell elsewhere sat in that finished basement in silence for a while, until Jimmy got up and socked his fist hard into his palm. He got up and hugged Porter and they held each other like athletes who'd scored a goal, but joyless. He left.

I had said that I just wasn't going to tell him, and I thought about it a lot before I telephoned him. By then, everything that had been was no more.

It wasn't simple bitterness that made me pick up the receiver. If what happened was both our responsibility, it was something consequential in his life—a momentous lesson he was owed to have. By then, all things told, it was clear to me that he was no longer—but perhaps had never been—the person I thought I knew. And yet, I'm guilt-ridden still to think I hadn't responded, in a way, enough to how seriously stricken he had become. Ellen Dolland notwithstanding.

I phoned him to see him, which I'd never done before. He'd been the one who would phone me, so he must have sensed from the start that there was something important that he had to know. I think he must have been visited by an intuition of what it might be. He was in an uneasy mood when he arrived, where I sat at a table in Kanter's candy store on Linden Boulevard, at the back of the store, in shadow, although it was a beautiful day outside.

Had I ordered anything? I just said no.

A malted? Jimmy's starting to talk with the offer of a malted made me more ill at ease. As if this could pass as another pleasant encounter embellished with a treat. I went along: vanilla.

Back at the counter, the malted machine whirled, filling a moment of silence.

"I was pregnant," I blurted

He didn't answer.

I held fire for a long moment.

"It's not for you to worry." My voice then suddenly took me to a different place. Suddenly I felt that I was talking to a stranger now—to someone I'd brought in from outside to inform him of what was no longer his concern.

"It's over!" I finally burst out.

"What?" His face frightened me.

"Yes but—"

It became clear to him.

"Why didn't you tell me?"

"How would that have changed anything? Everything is over!" I blurted.

He covered his ears with his hands, as if noise was raining down, but we were silent for a long moment. I could say nothing more.

He got up.

He ran out of the store.

It was over.

I write this story to know truth: about happening and to understand as best we can, what happens. At that moment, I was happy. Elated. On the landscape of my way ahead, I could foresee sun and a rainbow. Distantly, too distantly for an acceptable comparison, and even selfishly—you can condemn a thought, but thoughts come before they're condemned—I thought of the lucky ones who came back from the horror of war and overcame it. I drank the malted, and it tasted good.

Grandma wasn't through. The most critical happening since my father's death had come into our lives—our little family's life—and she felt anguish tormenting her soul to use a noun that still fitted her vision of the world. Grandma went to mass, although faith was something no longer safely imbedded in that soul. In the world's whirlwind of threats impending on everyone, the stubborn intrusion of faith was not to be thrown away on the wind because nothing else could offer an explanation for the "why." Faith was there for her, a kind of retained afterthought of a relieving possible, without deep conviction. But what she had to go by most of all, was love that was as natural and undeniable to her as a bodily function. Love for those close to her. For me. Love beyond analysis. Unassailable.

My mother, the nurse who'd been a repeated witness of blatant disaster, faced life by blocking out contemplation of whys. She'd just hit back. To cure, to save. Being a nurse was, if you like, her defining, existential answer to a question she willed to give no more thought.

But Grandma wasn't through. It was all too critical for her to be easily at rest.

My Grandma went back to see Lyons. She came with a kind of excuse. There'd been no mention of his fee. He threw the idea away, almost angrily.

"You ran a risk in your own life, doctor, in an important sense," she said gently. The law…"

"My own life was not what the matter was."

"I'm not sure that we thanked you enough."

"You know," he said, "we've intervened in life, and not inconsequentially. We did what we did, stopped something in nature. That's what doctors do—they do a lot of combat with nature and not always is it easy to know that what you do is in some overlooked sense what you had to do. I do not want to talk about it anymore. We came, all of us, all but one of us, to the belief that we were saving Erin's life—her life ahead. I met the boy. He is deeply wounded and can't seem to handle. I don't want to talk about it anymore."

She hadn't an answer. He'd said what she'd put together in her own mind. And coming here again had given her the confirmation. She felt relief.

"Is it intrusive to talk about you, Dr. Lyons?" She dared. "I want to tell you that you're greatly appreciated here. I'm a busybody with people. You're admired. But Alex—Alex Franklin was my good friend—already told me how he admired you.

And from him that was something more profound than an easy compliment."

He smiled. She had got him to that.

"Are you happy here?" she consequently asked.

"I have problems," he said, "...not about here and nothing to go public with and compromise the admiration. It assuages."

"I hope that you would count on me as a friend, as the friend you've been, Cato, just as Alex was."

"The boy," Lyons, was driven back there. "I am sure that he is not capable of being anything good in Erin's life now. It's not his fault, I mean he's not right in his mind...where he's been. I think that he should not see her anymore. She'll risk ruining her own life again, trying to help his."

"They were very close, very close, from the time they were little. Her father was killed you know. He was such a great comfort to her then," she said. You know, at one moment in all this, I felt moved to see Jimmy and ask him if what he really felt was love for her."

"That's not something I believe open to him now," he said. "I'd say he's too angry. Too much anger in him to have room for love. He should not even go near her anymore."

৵

Jimmy couldn't think of how long he'd been walking. That thought hadn't been one in the jumble in his mind, and now he found himself in the middle of the road, faced with a pile of construction stuff on Horace Harding Boulevard, where they were cutting a branch onto an expressway. Progress. He was in a *now* world that for a moment gave him the comforting illusion of having left behind the jumbled one he'd left. To go where? In his hand, he had a paper bag containing a pint bottle of scotch for the ceremony he'd decided on and since he'd drunk half of it on his way there, it had set loose, rather than calmed a confusion in his mind, of thoughts in and out of consciousness. All distraught.

A Dugan's Bakery truck came across Jimmy walking in the busy road. The driver stopped, looked out his window, amused.

"What's with your walking?"

"I could use a lift."

Jimmy saw that he was gray-looking and too old to be driving a truck. He climbed in.

"Walking is the best thing for your health in this world. I walk all the time. You think I sit on my butt in this truck every day?"

"You want me to get out?"

"I can use the company. Where you headed?"

"Saint John's Cemetery. Middle Village. By Elmhurst."

"You're on my route. I pass it all the time. You got relatives there?"

"I've got someone."

"Son, the greatest walker the world has known is out there. Say hello."

"To?"

"Edward Payson Weston, believe it, his real moniker. Walked across America. Walked up and down England. Walked from

Boston, Massachusetts to Washington. To Lincoln's inauguration. The President shook his hand."

The driver was silent for a moment, before he said, "A lowlife taxi driver in a hurry ran him over on a street in Brooklyn. It was what killed him. They got him a wheel chair because there was no way he was going to walk again, and he had nothing else to do—age ninety. Taxi drivers have to make a living, but they don't have to kill people to do it."

They arrived at the cemetery. This was the place.

"Say hello," the driver insisted, as Jimmy thanked him for the ride.

He walked around. All those dead Catholics, after years of getting up for masses and doing confessions, and here's their situation. He passed a corner which, from the names that he could recognize, seemed reserved for murdered Mafiosi. Then he came upon the famous walker. A non-acclamatory stone. Just "March 15, 1839 to May 12, 1929."

"Hello," Jimmy said. He took the bottle of scotch he'd been holding in the paper bag, waved a salute to Edward Payson Weston, and drank.

Without much trouble he found the grave that he'd come for, from the map the gate keeper gave him.

He held out his pint—as in a toast—and drank again.

"How you doing, P.J.?"

"You've got to believe it, P.J., I had this ride on a Dugan's truck, the old guy went on about a guy who was killed by a taxi."

"I thought of all the people we saw killed and the ones we

killed…I didn't invite him into knowing our world. His was about wearing out shoes and bread and cupcakes."

He drank again.

"The ride smelled good…like Danish. You wouldn't know. You're down there. Know what? There's a lot people these days thinking about digging deeper than graves and putting down concrete rooms. Getting ready for there's going to be a Russian A-bomb soon. For the next war. Go figure…

A little more left. He sipped.

"You're all right now. I'm messed up now."

"It's like…my thoughts are peeing in my head like I'm wetting my pants. No control. No lock and load. These thoughts come in before my brain thinks them over. And quick."

"Anyway…you are safe in your designated place in this world, P.J."

Nothing more to say. His mind was sodden with the scotch.

The pint was empty.

"I'll come back. What are friends for?"

The afternoon in Middle Village, Queens, among clean little clapboard houses, was fading.

This is how I can still see it all happening and what I really saw as they both always come back to me mingled and wake me from sleep, even after we knew what did happen. There were no patients waiting. Cato Lyons was in the living room listening to the radio, tuned to WQXR.

When I came in to do my filing, it was still playing. Wagner, like a dire, coincidental backdrop, Hagan's bellowing. I remembered that Lyons appreciated the force of Dionysius in Wagner, but he admired far more the glory of reason rendered sensual in Mozart. I know because I remember overhearing him defending to Father Maloney the ill-fated young genius, after Albert Einstein had written demeaningly about his music, calling "K. 537" Mozart imitating Mozart. Wagner came over loud enough for Lyons not to have heard the doorbell, when he saw the person on the threshold of his living room. His door was never locked. It was someone he knew. Lyons may have made little of the person's walking in on him and asked him to come in and sit down and held out his hand.

A hand of friendship was apparently struck first—perhaps the police saw something revelatory about that to go on. And then something the person had in his hand came down on Cato Lyons' head. It didn't kill him right away, but threw him to the floor.

Just then, the Doctor's phone began to ring.

Father Maloney had decided to ring up Lyons to get together. The phone kept ringing. When he got Lyons on the other end, his voice was slurred and inexpressive. "I hope that you're all right Cato," Maloney said. "Why don't you lie down?" He didn't allow himself to say, "And sleep it off," but what should he have said or done? He believed the Doctor, in his bout against alcohol, had badly lost a round. Going over there would have been an imposition and maybe an unforgiveable embarrassment. He said it twice:

"You'll feel better I'm sure if you'd just lie down." The phone clicked at the other end. As if Lyons were either offended or had taken the advice.

I came into the house just a while later. Too late. I heard Mary screaming.

Gus Loburg was standing beside her, catatonic, where Lyons had crawled to his office, blood all around—a pool of blood.

An ambulance from Mary Immaculate was screaming next. People had gathered in a hush. Mary came out, stunned and sobbing.

Gus Loburg came out next and he was able to murmur something in which "*Gott*" was a frequent word. He saw Minna and rushed up to her and grabbed her in his arms. "*Gott in Himmel!*"

Then the men in white brought the doctor out on a stretcher, with a blanket over him. It covered his face.

࿇

People came from all over with their cameras and photographed the house. Some people went and cut flowers from under Dr. Lyons' sun porch window, too fast for a cop to have chased them off without their souvenirs. Someone said something about Lepke, and a half-dozen men and women went and photographed the Siegals' house, while Ivor and Blanche hovered in their sun porch. The news of what happened reached the City. Al Willard, the *Daily News* photographer famous for illustrating crime stories came with his Speed Graphic, but he was too late to get a shot of Dr. Lyons being carried out, and he mentioned to someone among the bystanders that it was a wasted assignment. Willard did crime scenes with the corpse still there in a pool of blood on the street and his police friends would let him cross their line and exclusively shoot the scene—the body still warm. Anyone, he said, could have been handed this job. Willard lived close by in Queens Village. He shot Lyons' house, gave a couple of Speed Graphic plates to the guy who had come after him on a motorcycle, and drove home. His day was over.

The event was not yet over. As one of the policemen who had taped off the house told the reporter who'd come with Willard, "We have zero yet on the perp but we're working on it a lot."

The latest arrival was Cato's Dorothy. There was a guy with her behind the wheel of a car. No taxi this time.

She argued with the cop who barred her way. "I'm the wife," she insisted, "the house is mine."

She claimed that she had personal things in there.

The policeman restrained her with his hand on her arm. She shook him off and turned back to the car. Someone with a Brownie took her picture as she got in. Then, while the man with the camera looked up at the sun with an air of gratitude for the light, the guy behind the wheel of her car pulled away with a screech.

I saw all this standing beside Father Maloney, who'd come too late for his bestowing last rites. Lyons had indeed become his friend. He was looking bleak, bitter even, angry, as if once again he'd been confronted on the path of Job, with inexplicable injustice, and he'd, once again, have to argue himself back to his faith…

⚘

Two detectives had been waiting at the gates of Calvary Cemetery in Woodside, after the ceremony in which people sang a hymn while Warren Porter wept silently, holding a little coffin in his arms, until a workman took it and lowered it into the ground. A fellow Black in an Army Air Force uniform hugged Jacqueline while she sobbed beside the hole. The soldier turned away to look keenly at the Whites among the mourners.

I stood behind with Victoria Rose. I felt weak again. I thought that I'd faint. Behind Porter, there was Jimmy King and Sanford Rose, anger mixed with grief on those faces.

The detectives went off with Porter as he was leaving through the gates.

⚘

The police were hoping for a quick close to the case. There was Loburg whom I'd found standing over Lyons lying on the floor. Mary confirmed that Loburg had raced in when he heard her screaming. She'd been vacuuming on the second floor and never saw the intruder. In any case, Loburg had been just pulling into his driveway from a visit to his chiropractor to have lunch home with Minna. They eliminated him as the perpetrator. They had a lead when going over Lyons' papers; they found a mention of money owed, and it was not a negligible sum—four-thousand dollars. When they questioned Mary, she revealed that there were afternoons that Cato Lyons would take off after studying racing sheets. The race track didn't at all fit my image of Dr. Lyons. Looking back, I see a morbid sense to his habit. The world he'd known was a world of grave hostility. Gambling may have been a little like his playing Russian roulette, defying it with playing for concrete victories. He was no longer the doctor he'd been and his mastery of life was badly damaged. The horses—choosing winners with skill and care— meant another mastery; the narrow, and in a sense easy, way for him to hope to get the better of the world. So it seems to me, as I try to explain this surprising thing, but who can really fathom all the things that drive people to somewhere, in some way irrational or contradictory as often as it is not. Think of those compelled by an obsession that drives them to avoid danger to their lives in by stepping on sidewalk cracks.

She'd understood that he was always going to the track at Belmont, close by. A name was written with a sum on a pad near Lyons' phone. Beringer. The police knew a Beringer who had a record as a cruel loan shark. A beating might have been all he had scheduled to remind about a debt, which his emissary had ill-executed. So there was Beringer to get ahold of. He wasn't where he lived, and they sent out a BOLO to find him. Mary had also told them of a recent day when she heard the doctor quarreling with a man who came without an appointment, shouting at Lyons, "You're going to give the divorce!" Mary thought they may have scuffled. The man rushed out without even looking at her. His separated wife's lover? Why not? She'd already turned up nasty, but the police had trouble running her down to get to the guy; nobody had taken the license plate number of the car she'd come in.

Meanwhile the third lead was close to home, and they jumped on it right away. Was Porter angry? Yes. Did his anger at the doctor who'd misdiagnosed his daughter make sense? Would things have turned out differently for the kid in any case? No. But you don't need to go and kill somebody for a well-reasoned motive. He was angry and maybe out of his mind with anger. Anger at the death for which he saw no relief except to pin it on a protagonist? He had a grievance against the Whites of the neighborhood. The police went forward to try a confession and wrap it all up.

They'd picked him up for questioning at the cemetery where he was burying his baby. Porter, with what he'd gone through with his daughter was in no shape to deal with that. He was not, as they would put it, "a cooperative witness."

Hadn't he already killed a lot of people? As if, in a sense, his license hadn't expired. His boss confirmed that he was at work that day, but since the fellow was colored too, they had reason to suspect he was covering for him out of solidarity of race.

What was he like at work? Did he seem angry at the doctor? Yes, he was. He'd read up that there were polio patients who responded to treatment when caught in time. They kept him in a cell, and they kept questioning him in turns—each detective practicing the psychology of his own technique until they got tired and resorted to the classic one. They "waffled" him, as the cops like to call it.

That did it. Porter hit back. And he was good at it. It took four policemen to beat him down to his knees. They booked him on resisting arrest, which meant that a writ of habeas corpus couldn't apply.

Jacqueline came to visit with a lawyer—a very young man who was dedicated to justice. I don't know how she got hold of him. The police found his manner aggressive, and somewhat amusing. He got nowhere, while for two days more, Porter was waffled; the classic technique was with a folded newspaper.

Then the lawyer was back with an older man in better clothes, a lawyer who spoke sternly to the cops before he met with them in a closed room. The two lawyers took Porter home.

꿎

A requiem may be held in the Roman Catholic Church for someone who was not a Catholic but who had been baptized. Whether that qualified Cato Lyons, a lapsed convert, who'd after all been named at birth after a pagan, or not, Father Maloney was who he was, and he did what he did. He called it a funeral service in his notice outside the church, and everyone was invited to attend what would be his shortened ceremony.

When he finished his final prayer, there was a moment of silence, when he seemed waiting to know what he should say that was personal. There was suddenly the sound of rapping on the stone floor of the church. A man with a cane in his white gloved hand was walking forward. He wore a Marine dress blues uniform—the formal one. He had the age, the medals, and the dignified air of a onetime high officer.

He asked the priest to speak, and Maloney held out his hand in a gesture of welcome.

"I live in Chicago," the Marine said, "and when I read about what happened here, I hoped that there would be a ceremony to come to, and I've come. I didn't know Commander Lyons well at all. I encountered him only once, and I can say that it was at an important moment in my life. He was bent over in a tent lit by a kerosene lamp, and they were bringing him, all day and night, torn lives, shattered lives, and he would put them together again, mine among them.

"He looked like he was going without sleep. He looked like a ghost. But that ghost was our angel, and as incredibly tired as he was, his hands held steady and you could say worked miracles.

"I can't say anything more that would mean anything more. He deserved a great medal. I don't know if he got one, I think someone said he did, but I don't know which it was. He was not the kind of man, from what I could perceive, to whom a medal would be his motivation. I can't say anything that would mean more." No one else spoke. But there were many of Cato Lyons' patients there. Among them I saw Salvatore, the former sexton, and Mary in the last pew. My grandmother and my mother looked devastated.

Mary was sobbing again.

I saw Jimmy, who'd come late, in the doorway.

ELEVEN

All day long, he hadn't come home nor made contact. In the morning, Pastor King was burdened with a premonition of deep gravity and yet a ray of hope—that he might find his son gone to a kind of sanctuary, the place filled with good in his life, ever since childhood. He waited through supper the next day and then got into his car…

That afternoon Edith King was waiting for me in her car in front of my house when I came home. I saw her face: Something had happened to Jimmy. She looked imploringly at me. I got in beside her.

"Erin," she asked, "Can we talk?"

We drove to the same candy store, Kanter's, where I'd last been with Jimmy. She ordered coffee, and I did the same; anything else among the usual treats there now would have had a congenial connotation of enjoyment, which was in no way in order.

"We don't know what's happened to Jimmy," she said.

"I saw him come in during the funeral," I said, "but he was gone by the time I'd gone out."

"And you don't know where he is?" The grief in her voice worsened because she didn't doubt what I'd said.

I told her I didn't know that he was missing.

"For more than a day…"

"I think he cares a lot for you," she said.

There were things I could tell her that I never would. That it would do her no good at all to know. I said something ordinary:

"If I hear from him I'll certainly let you know."

"Thank you," she said.

That was the only time that I would ever be with her. But it was as if invisible beams of recognition had touched. She may have intuited that I was a force for good in her son's life. I hoped so, and I felt about her as I would have felt about my grandmother—that the two of them incarnated the mighty, authentic love of mothers.

It was now as if changing places could have the power to change time. Run it back differently.

Jimmy had indeed boarded a Greyhound to Chestertown and walked the rest of the way. Being up there now was like pulling a blanket over his head, there in his own room, against the ghosts around his bed. Awake, he sat on the porch, rocking his chair with a beat like a cradle's, until he saw the headlights of the gray Packard beaming on the porch.

They spoke late into the night until they ran out of memories, and then there was a long, deep, comforting silence, as if in their minds' eyes a bright, beloved succession of living had all unreeled, and then, and in the silence that followed, as if they were outside time or in asylum from it, until Jimmy spoke the non-rescindable, and the soldierly pastor wept.

James King Sr. drove home in the morning. The police called him and said they were investigating the murder of Lyons and they were asking anyone who'd known him for clues. Pastor King told them that Jimmy was away, but would make contact when he came home soon.

When Jimmy was back, two days later, he had made up what was left of his mind and faced the consequences of what had turned out.

He walked into the 105th precinct and confessed.

EPILOGUE

t was, he believed, a child. It was, he believed, *his* child. No matter what argument in the ongoing arguments about the existential definition of what or who it was, what happened was about who he was. He was what he'd become. A fallen angel among the many whom those times undid, each by way of a dire concatenation of danger.

It took me a long time to be able to see him. By then I was well into a new life—still single, still the one person and not the new person with the paired presence of a new other. Not that, until I met Walter and the bond happened; a fulfillment through another definition of what we do in being human. My lifelong marriage.

I waited years with this manuscript still unfinished. In one sense, it was too uncomfortably close to what it brought to life. I waited for me to decant what had settled, to delve in the source that comes back to writers in a gaggle of secrets, truths, counter-truths, and even artful lies. Maybe I wanted, with cooled distance, to be sure of what was right in what I perceived, learned, intuited, and give their account to this version of life. Maybe selfishly. Maybe deservedly selfish.

I took the Grand Central train from New York City, up to Dannemora, above Chestertown, the institution that used to be dedicated to house the criminally insane.

It was a shock, although why should it not have been? The athlete's frame gone flabby, from the food they gave him—and the medication.

He smoked without stop, blowing smoke rings against the glass separating us. He wouldn't speak…

I came back a second time. Jimmy came out to receive me without saying a word. He was silent for a moment, and I felt that for all that mattered, he wasn't there for me…until, at last, he spoke into the phone receiver. He said, with a smile that came across as the opposite of what we feel to be a smile: "Do you think we could ever have happily married?" I couldn't reach back with an answer. He shook his head no over and over, while he couldn't speak.

He seemed to have wanted to relieve me of the answer with that—I like to believe that he'd settled things in his mind for my sake—and on the same wavelength he said: "Don't come back Erin."

I thought I heard him say it again, as he turned away.

And he got up to leave the room. For a moment, standing there, in my agitated mind, I heard it like an echo:

He said again: "Don't look back Erin." The voice, as he stepped toward his door was no longer close to the glass that had been between us. It was like the cry of someone calling back from being carried away by a torrent, to where no one could be close enough to save him.

"Keep going!"

There had been moments when I felt strongly that I had been with someone deeply grieved but normal, while I knew that the "workups" on him proved the contrary.

As I was leaving the grounds, that last time, I saw a familiar face. Warren Porter was going in. I don't know even now whether he noticed me, or whether in his mind I was one of the neighbors he'd known, all of us be damned, and he'd ignored me. I felt suddenly very awkward, with his whole story coming back to me. I walked on silently, too uncomfortable about what abrasion in his memory my greeting might provoke for him. I kept walking while he went in with a carton of cigarettes in his hand...

I went out to Pinelawn the next day, where among all the white stones of dead heroes, Commander Cato Lyons had his given place. No bigger one than elsewhere, but someone had covered it recently with still-fresh flowers. I, of course, couldn't say who had placed them there. Back in Tarawa, there had been I don't know how many Marines who might someday give this testimony of their gratitude for their lives. I thought of Mary and her husband who revered the good doctor who had succeeded their long-revered Alex Franklin. I thought of Edith King...

For a moment, standing there in the warm sunlight that evoked a benevolent state of the universe, I imagined Cato's wife, come repentant from a tearing apart that ended perhaps worse, and leaving all those red roses.

My last thought was hard to express, but I spoke it as if he might somewhere hear:

"You gave me my freedom, and it cost you your life."

⁓

Cambria Heights, as we knew it, is gone. The past. Yet the past, all things said, is part of an endless coil of being that encloses our world, and you don't need Einstein to tell you that what happens always is. The classic metaphor, of course, that illustrates the major downside of it all is the Garden of Eden. Evil creates more evil, on and on, whether you really do believe the quaint story and that this has all happened, or you just say forever…on and on. But in this world in which Sanford Rose devoted himself to a hopelessly poisonous ideal for changing it—great things other than sin, I mean love and empathy, do get passed on as we make our fumbling way, with the impulse to lessen the communal calamities of being born. That's what I believe: nothing more than a kind of faith. Call me a positive-thinking Manichean, if what I declare about myself matters here anyway…

War came again. In just a few years, and my mother—loyal to the life she'd decreed to define herself—went off to it again. She expired in the dormitory attached to her hospital in Seoul. In her sleep, of overwork and a weak heart. Beside her iron bed, a picture of her and her one and only man, together in their youth in what looked like an amusement park, sat on her night table.

Beside one of me in a cap and gown.

Pastor King and Edith retired near Chestertown, after the time it took a new minister to take over the parish. He was perhaps as ashamed as aggrieved. But I believe from what I can finally put together that he dearly loved his son. His former church would dwindle in parishioners as religion dwindled in the decades that followed, until, with the change in the ethnicity of the neighborhood, it gave over to a Black Baptist congregation and was reborn with song.

Father Maloney stayed on at the parish of Sacred Heart until he retired at a Catholic old age home in North Carolina. His church prevailed with new Catholic parishioners. The priest who ultimately replaced him was an immigrant from Haiti.

Warren Porter went home from the police station to where he could no longer feel at home. His luck, what seemed left of it, had it that one of his fellow airmen found him an apartment in a two-family house in a largely Black neighborhood of Jamaica, where he would go on—having got a new job as an auto mechanic—to create a used car business with a G.I. loan, and buy a comfortable house.

Sanford Rose endured a more heart-wrenching change. His canvassing for candidates of the American Labor Party, and the "subversive" thoughts he passed onto his students, got him fired as a high school teacher, in the McCarthy era that followed that time in Cambria. With no fortune being part of his credo, he moved to where real estate was cheaper in Jamaica. Warren Porter immediately gave him the job of a salesman in his used car dealership. It was not consistent with Rose's convictions about what a person should do in life, but—able also to afford a more confidence-inspiring wardrobe—he prospered from the reputation that spread widely of his and Warren's rare honesty, in a business renowned for the opposite. Jacqueline Porter ran for Congress on the Democratic ticket and won the office she held for years before she retired. Sanford's Victoria found a loft to conduct her dancing classes. A good half-dozen of her Black students would go on to be professional, including Errol

Clarke, whose troupe would gain renown performing through-out the world.

Gustav Loburg retired to live with Minna in Karlsruhe, which would be totally restored, while their twins stayed in America. Iris was with them when those two brothers saw them off at the Pier of the Holland-American line. The war was long over. Iris had always had a kind word for Minna.

Louis "Lepke" Buchalter, CEO of Murder Incorporated had been electrocuted, but his career had been prosperous enough for his widow, the Siegals' daughter, to enable her parents to end their lives in a luxurious nursing home in Florida.

⌘

All gone, the place that was, but what is there now is another as modestly idyllic. I went back to Cambria Heights from where I live in Manhattan, near NYU, where Walter, my husband—my soulmate—teaches. It was in 2014. Porter and Rose, were they not gone, would rejoice in this neighborhood where Blacks moved when Whites ran away. They'd see simple dreams real-ized again, by people unchained from a long past of calamity and hardship—realized, come concretely true, with their manicured lawns, their flower beds, and their little "Tudor" houses, many renovated into images of more elaborate prosperity. Cambria Heights is an African-American neighborhood, but not a ghetto. Many Whites have gone back to profit from the rare look and feel of something like the personality of a small town within the borders of the big city of New York.

My grandmother, with my living away at graduate school and my mother gone off, stayed in our house full of memories, becoming the last White person on the street until things changed after the seventies. She lived happily where she chose she would die, babysitting for her neighbors, into her nineties.

Cambria Heights had been largely spared the polio epidemic. The Liu and Porter children's afflictions turned out to be rare exceptions there, during that season in Queens while the disease raged throughout the nation in a way unmatched since 1916, with 22,371 afflictions. But the fight to destroy polio is finally close to victory. With vaccinations all over the world, the number of reported cases everywhere, as I finally write, are a few hundred...

She wrote, "The End." I feel compelled to add my ending: my beginning in our joined lives. I, Iris Two.

I'm the second Iris with the name she gave me in honor of her grandmother, and this is another gift, which I send out for her into the world: Erin's "true novel" in the papers that she left me. The offspring of her talented mind...

My mother died still young and having been long lovely. Not by any calendar, but I say that in every way, and because, despite the inexorable change, Erin never changed from the avid awareness that I always knew her to have.

I call her by her first name as I have since the days that she took me home. I call her like a friend, which she declared, in her sentient way of knowing, more intimate, more personal, than saying "Mom." It resonates with the memory of the cherished friend that with all else my mother was, as mothers not always are, and she chose to call me Iris, after her beloved grandmother, even though the nuns had baptized me Carol.

These pages were in an envelope with her effects that she left in my name.

Erin Burke had made a lot of people happy with her children's stories and had won a prize for the genre. Simple but richly imagined fantasies, like contemporary fairy tales, in which little kids are encouraged willfully to suspend disbelief—to nurture their imaginations rather than their cognizance of the world as it is, as if they had time for that trying confrontation. I know nothing of her having ever written anything else before this about "the real world" and with it she left me a letter.

She wrote:

"This oddly fugal thing, buried, unburied, and reburied in a drawer, is a story—*my* story:

"Call this my 'true novel.' I have learned, imagined, and surmised, and, I've fleshed out a long metaphor of what we do with and to each other—my confection of reality added to the substantive world."

She wrote:

"I've known the awe of the ordinary…"

I see Erin still—over and over. Her memory is my cherished

property. I see her with her heart-wrenching chemo scalp where she'd had that lovely red hair that had never turned gray. She never got old. But with all I've said and all I remember, when I close my eyes, the image of her that comes back more often than any other, is of that moment where I'm standing in the parlor of the Little Daughters, an undernourished Cambodian kid not pretty either, as funny maybe as Jimmy's poor dog Moe. And she beams at me. And she looks back and smiles at Walter, behind her, with a look of "Yes?" As if she didn't know that Walter could never say no to her. (He had warned her in the elevator, "Don't you get into religion with those ladies.")

She'd come to be my mother—her only possible child. To take the orphan me home, as she did. And hold me all those times that she would. As if squeezing away my memory of all the horror of what I'd been through (enough said), and about which I couldn't, as an infant, comprehend, and as if her tight embrace was a paradigm of our being physically attached.

The End

Other Books by Joanne and Gerry Dryansky

Fatima's Good Fortune

Fortune's Second Wink

Satan Lake

Chant'd'Adieu

The Heirs

Other People

Non Fiction:

Coquilles, Calva and Crème

About the Authors

J oanne and Gerry Dryansky, Queens-bred, have lived much of their lives in Paris, while Gerry was successively foreign correspondent, magazine editor, and magazine contributor for American publications, for which Joanne was his secret weapon. Leaving behind *Condé Nast*, they have since devoted themselves wholly to their love of making up stories together.

Printed in the USA
CPSIA information can be obtained
at www.ICGtesting.com
JSHW022328140824
68134JS00019B/1359